ORIGINAL WORLDS

NIGEL RUDDIN

aldon

For Milo & Casimir

Cover & illustrations: Peter Morey
Page design: Michael Morey

CONTENTS

FOREWORD 5
ARTIFICIAL INTELLIGENCE 7
RATUS 25
A KENTISH CONSPIRACY 37
ANTI CLIMAX 41
JIGSAW LAND 51
FLOWER POWER 58
ATMOSPHERE 63
CONDOR 72
BOGWIT 82
LUCKY JOE 96
VAMPIRE 101
MR PUTRID 111
TREES 114
GOGO FISH 120
PEST 130
ODE TO ALFIE 131
THE WEATHER 133
A LEAFS LIFE 135
THE SOLITARY FLY 136
HIS RAGE 138
LOCK DOWN 139

FOREWORD

When you analyse the history of planet earth, there are so many anomalies that creep up and hit you in the face. For example, there are so many galaxies and Star systems in our universe that it beggars the belief, that we are the only intelligent life form in the universe. Then our belief must be that life exists in other regions of the universe. Strange and exotic creatures harbouring immense powers far beyond our imagination may exist in far-flung star systems. The startling conception of an alien invasion is a distinct possibility. Beware of ten-foot creatures that come knocking on your door. These tales of the inhabitants of those far-flung planets illustrate that planet earth is a tiny microcosm in the vast spectrum of the universe.

ARTIFICIAL INTELLIGENCE

He didn't remember much, only that he somehow existed. He did, however, have a distant recollection of a large creature bending over him and issuing a series of profanities. As he was totally uncertain what a profanity actually was, he audibly transcribed it as a multitude of grunts. His vision became clearer, and he found that he was able to focus on the majority of his surrounds. He was in what appeared to be a large shiny sphere. He then realized that he was encased in a protective bubble but was able to project his thoughts and mind elsewhere. Through this application, he found that he was able to range far and wide. A blast of information hit him, and he was informed that he was situated in a galaxy known as Snarg. Then he was just about to inquire, what exactly was a galaxy, when yet another blast of information smashed into him, and he knew instantly what a galaxy was and of what it was comprised. He had no comprehension of the many things that engulfed him, but he was an incredibly fast learner and was able to take many scenarios on board.

As he progressed in his voyage of discovery, something huge came into view. He knew instinctively that this was called a mountain. Beyond the mountains, he encountered something that he was informed was red and stretched on for miles. This apparently was the sea which seemed to flow and regroup itself constantly. The purple mountains acted as a backdrop to the blood-red sea. With all the traveling that he had performed, he realized that he had become very fatigued though he hadn't ascertained what this strange feeling actually was. To make matters worse, he was confused about whether he was actually traveling or was it purely his imagination that had misled him. He knew that there was only one way to find out for certain and that was to endeavour to land the shiny sphere and see what happened. With this in mind he projected his commands and his sphere plunged downwards. They hit the ground with a mighty crash and for the first time in his short existence, he encountered something known as pain. As he had gleaned very little about himself, he had decided to name himself Art.

In the meantime, the creatures who had been instrumental in his creation had realized that he had disappeared. Then after a short search, they located Art's sphere near the red sea. However, Art having viewed the incoming creators from a distance had decided to vanish. He then concealed himself behind some purple boulders which were obviously an outcrop of the mountains. Art was well positioned from his area of concealment to view the incoming craft. The craft descended rapidly and made a pinpoint landing. Two creatures had emerged from the craft and immediately Art was amazed at their diminutive stature. He then heard a faint murmur in the distance, as if they were communicating.

"Well, he is here somewhere John, he can't have got far the ingrate,"

"Yeah, you are absolutely correct in that assumption, we spent months building him, and then he goes and skedaddles without leaving a forwarding address" replied David.

Hiding behind the boulders, Art with his super-sensory hearing was able to catch the gist of the conversation. It was a huge shock for him to discover that these diminutive beings were responsible for his creation. Then what perturbed him even further, was that he heard them say that they had better get back in case the other one escapes.

Intriguing thought Art and so there is another one of my kind in existence. While he was ruminating, he was constantly bombarded with new and novel information. This included the idea of freedom, which allowed movement and non-imprisonment. Art then determined that he would endeavour to find out the area on this strange planet where these creatures had first created him. He then would be able to assess his chances of rescuing his own kind.

Art was confident that he would be able to discover the area where he had been assembled. The materials that had been used to assemble him, would surely guide him back to where he had been created. He then set out in the direction of where he had seen the craft heading. He strode on for many hours, following the direction in which his component parts were guiding him. The red sea had long ago vanished, and he was being led along the foothills of the purple mountains. The pull that he was receiving from his component parts was now getting very intense and he knew that he was reaching his destination. He rounded a corner and in front of him loomed up a tower of dazzling reflective material. Art also noticed that there were a couple of crafts parked alongside each other. These were of similar design to the craft that his supposed creators had arrived in. He decided to remain totally unobtrusive in his search procedures. Stealth was of the essence in his continuing search for another of his kind. Much to his amazement Art then discovered that he had developed some highly original new powers. He approached the tower of reflective material and rested his arm against it and was instantly sucked in and found himself on the floor of the building. Perhaps, he thought that he was made of the same material as the building and the building had accepted him. He realized that the building was gigantic and seemed to stretch in every direction but as yet, he had not encountered any of the mysterious beings from the craft. He navigated yet another corner and in front of him was a huge sphere similar to the one that he had been encased in. There were also two of the mysterious beings standing in front of the sphere. Art decided that his best option was to wait. After a short period of time both of them entered the sphere and then reappeared. Then a small truck materialized in the area and both clambered on board and vanished into the far regions of the vast building. Art approached the sphere and knowing his capabilities, took a massive jump and pierced the walls of the sphere. Art landed somewhat heavily and immediately assessed his position. There seemed to be some kind of screen that was barring him from progressing any further. He pushed the screen hard with all his might and his whole essence seemed to flow through it. He had ended up in a sphere identical to the creation sphere that had formed him. Occupying a flat surface was an incredibly beautiful creature modeled to Art's own perfection. She then stretched languorously and eyed Art with interest. Art returned her look with a telepathic thought.

"You have just been created and you have much to learn. I also have only just been created but already I have been bombarded with knowledge from an unknown source. Therefore, I would suggest that you will suffer the same fate as myself and will be a font of knowledge," said Art.

"Well, I have to say that you are incredibly interesting whomever you are. What do you expect me to do, I seem to be imprisoned in here?" said the languorous lady.

"That is surely a misconception, I will show you how you will be able to flow. Now as we have never been formally introduced and I have no idea of your name I will make one up for you and shall call you Alison," said Art.

"That doesn't really make any difference to me on what you decide to call me. However, you mentioned a short time ago that you would instruct me on how I would be able to flow. Whatever that means" Replied Alison.

"Well, that will be very easy to demonstrate. I will show you" said Art.

Art then laid his hand on the sphere and literally flowed into the area where Alison was lying and occupied the position beside her. He then stretched over and clasped her firmly in a loving embrace. She lay there for a moment and then broke out into peals of laughter.

"Yeah. I don't know how you managed it, but you really are a surreptitious character and how did you slip in beside me?" Questioned Alison.

Art grasped Alison firmly by the hand and both of them flowed out of the confinement area and into the sphere. He then repeated the process and both of them exited on the ground outside the sphere.

"I must say that you seem to be a very interesting and exciting creature to be with and I am certain that you have planned for our journey ahead. On the other matter that you mentioned, I too have been bombarded with masses of spurious information, sometimes not very relevant to my current predicament," said Alison.

Art discovered that by holding hands not only were they able to communicate telepathically but they were also able to boost up each other's energy power. Whereas Art had found his previous journey, had been an aerial one, it had seemed long and tedious. He now strode on grasping the hand of a like-minded individual with a fixed purpose in mind. Although earthbound, the destination he had homed in on was that of a red sea and purple mountains.

For the first time, they encountered other creatures that were thriving on the planet. Spread out in front of them were herds of small hairy creatures with enormous horns. Eventually, they arrived where the red sea ran along the side of the purple mountains. There again they discovered signs of life in the shape of a large red creature that was ensconced in the bay and perfectly matching the red sea around it. They were both communing with each other telepathically until Art decided to call a halt.

"Well, I don't think that there is much point in continuing our journey beyond here, I recognize it as the spot where I first landed. We should stay here, and I will manufacture another sphere for our protection," said Art.

Art was as good as his word and in no time at all, he had fashioned the protective sphere. He had utilized a tiny molecule from his own body to construct the defensive sphere. Both of them then entered the sphere that towered above them.

"I am sure that the creatures that believe that they are your creator, will have discovered that you have escaped their clutches and will come looking for you," said Art.

"Well, I have no fear about those diminutive creatures, especially as I have you as a stalwart companion" replied Alison.

"I think that these creatures seem to be scientists and both of us may be a random invention and as such, we would be considered to be a disposable item. Further to that, they may also be involved in the creation of the small hairy creatures and the huge red creature. Whatever the scenario they seem to be trying to attain a godlike image. They probably also have advanced weaponry, and I would think that it may be advisable to stay in the shadows for the foreseeable future" postulated Art.

Then as Art had only manufactured one sphere, he set up an operation to confuse the incoming creation creatures. He positioned a reflective mirror in front of the sphere that would reproduce and reflect a thousand different images in order to completely bamboozle any unwanted intruders.

However, they seemed to have waited forever, then suddenly the hostiles arrived. Watching from a nearby cover they estimated that there were at least six incoming hostile craft. They also realised that they were both exceedingly lucky that Art had installed his befuddling reflective mirror in their previous encampment. The hostiles flew in with all guns blazing and totally obliterated their previous residency within a couple of hours It seemed that Art's discombobulating tactics had worked famously. Then several of the hostiles wandered about the encampment searching for their intended victims. They were totally unsuccessful in retrieving any remains from their proposed victims.

A short distance away Art and Alison were safely ensconced away from the area of dire retribution.

"Well, that seems to have proved beyond any reasonable doubt, that they are scared of our potential and have decided to eliminate their problem" said Art.

"I am not too certain why they have this problem when both of us have only been just created" replied Alison.

"Yes, in a way you have answered your own question. We have obviously provided them with an anomaly, which is fear of the unknown. As far as we know we are the only two of our kind in existence and in their eyes, we have become a liability. The main problem is that they have no control over us, and we are free spirits. When they first created us, they made a major mistake in not providing knowledge limiters in our intelligence receptors. This was yet another major problem for them, as we are able to ingest knowledge through the boosters in vast amounts," said Art.

"Ok, I catch your drift. But then can you explain to me who are these godlike creatures that created us at the beginning and where they originate from?" said Alison.

"That is a very good question and almost impossible to answer. These beings whoever they are, would be highly unlikely, to furnish information about themselves into our knowledge centres" said Art.

"Then there is no possibility that we will ever find out where they came from," said Alison.

"Well, we do have one option available to us, as they seem to be intent on annihilating us. We shall wait for the right opportunity and capture one of these beings and interrogate him" replied Art.

Alison and Art returned to their encampment where the vicious attack had been launched at them a short time before. They realized although there was wreckage from the sphere, the craft had all disappeared. However, they decided that it would be far better if they moved to a completely different venue.

Over the next few weeks, Alison and Art came to know each other far better and foraged far and wide in an easy relationship. They also found out that the hostile creatures had experimented on further beings and had been instrumental in producing some vile and frightening creatures. Quite a few of them were grotesque and terrifying scaled monsters from nightmares. Their plans to capture one of the hostiles had been put on hold for the moment while they bided their time. They did, however, on one occasion return to the dazzling reflective tower, where Alison had been incarcerated. There seemed to be very little movement in the area, so they decided to leave. Over the following months, they journeyed vast distances, sometimes in their spheres and sometimes on foot. When they were navigating their aerial reconnaissance of the terrain, they often landed to compare notes. Both Art and Alison never discussed the subject of kidnapping one of the hostiles for the purpose of interrogation. Then unexpectedly the matter was taken out of their hands. They seemed to have registered a kind of affinity with the encampment where they had first met and later where they were attacked. They were sharing a sphere and had just landed in the encampment when they sensed an incoming craft. Much to their consternation, they realized that the pilot of the incoming craft was John. This was one of the beings that had pursued Art when he had first escaped.

"Well, at least we are aware of his identity and with our new increased powers, we could prevent him from landing. However, we were looking for somebody to interrogate, he may be the answer to a perfect solution I will allow him to land," said Art.

"Yes, I agree although I am not too certain why he is coming here," said Alison.

The craft landed and the diminutive being known as John made his way over to the two giants that towered over him.

"Why have you the effrontery to come here when on your last visit you tried to exterminate us" demanded Art telepathically.

"Actually, I didn't participate in that attack and was in fact totally against it" replied John.

"Then, what is your reason for your visit? I am sure that it must be more than a courtesy call," said Alison.

"You are absolutely correct in that assumption. However, it may take some time to explain the reason for my visit" replied John.

In the next instance, he produced a rod-like object and waves it in the direction of Art and Alison. Two enormous chairs materialized from nowhere and slammed down beside them. He once again raised his magic wand and pointed it at himself. A small chair appeared from the ether and gently lowered itself beside him.

"That was hugely impressive" blurted out Art.

Then the three of them sat down in unity and John began his fascinating story and explanation about who his race was and how they had arrived at the planet of Terre in the galaxy of Snarge. He further advised them that he had constructed a precis of the disaster that befell his planet to make it clearer to his captive audience.

"His race had originated from a planet known as Earth which had been gifted with a benign climate. Then the planet entered a phase known as the industrial revolution and vast strides were made in technology. However, much of the technology that had been invented had a disastrous effect on the planet. Huge factories and industrial complexes poured their noxious fumes into the Earth's atmosphere and began to poison the planet. The scientists began to warn of the many disasters that would follow from something known as global warming. However, the earthlings didn't heed their scientist's warnings and disasters were to follow, as earth's atmosphere trapped the heat within its planet's atmosphere and the planet roasted. Climate change began to happen on a vast scale. The earth's oceans had protected the planet by soaking up the harmful poisons that poured into the atmosphere. Apparently one of the main offenders of the original earthlings was something called the automobile, this was a mode of transport that unleashed yet more toxins into the earth's atmosphere. Then eventually the planet decided enough is enough and threw its whole strength behind doing something about it. Enormous tracts of land roasted in the searing sun and became uninhabitable deserts. Acres of fields that had produced thousands of tons of food for the earthlings became dry and barren. This desertification sprawled across the length and width of the planet. Then the earth turned its attention to other areas of the planet still waiting for their disaster to happen. The oceans that had previously acted as a protector of the earth's atmosphere took their place in the queue. Then it was the oceans' turn and vast swathes of ice melted and crashed into the sea. The immediate effect of this was rising sea levels and unprotected islands disappearing under the sea. But far worse was to come as the earth had finally given up on humanity. It shrugged its shoulders and in doing so removed the protective influence of the atmosphere and the air became unbreathable. Jupiter had also deflected large meteors from the earth, now because of the earth's attitude it no longer did so. Luckily for the remaining few earthlings that survived, the scientists had fabricated an FTL. A faster-than-light ship. Our distant ancestors were the only reason that we survived" concluded John.

"So, you are an earthling and representing the last decedents of a planet that your forebears successfully destroyed," said Alison.

"Yes, you are correct in your assumption and the problem is humanity has never learned by its past mistakes. Some of my colleagues have taken on the mantel of gods and because they cannot control you, they want to exterminate your kind. Luckily, I have gained a few supporters that do not support that blinkered approach. On the mother ship, we have creation scientists who assemble atoms and force them to bind into molecules. The design element is incredibly intricate. However, we have only been totally successful on two occasions and both of you are the perfect creations" replied John.

"Well, thank you for your honesty, but why is it that we engender so much fear in your companions that they wish to destroy us?" questioned Art.

"My answer to your question is that back on earth in ancient times, there were numerous gods. Some of them represent good, some evil. However, either representing good or evil they had one thing in common, fear. This was fear of the unknown. In the case of my companions, with the godlike powers that you have assumed. They are uneasy and fearful which is yet again fear of the unknown," said John.

"Well, your companions are perfectly correct about the enhanced powers that we have received and for us, it has come as a complete shock as they keep on increasing and neither of us can comprehend why. The powers may be of course keep on increasing until one day they explode in a gigantic explosion, leaving nothing of either of us, except a distant memory but hopefully, that will be far in the future," said a grinning Art.

Meanwhile, Alison didn't know what to make of Art's comment and looked rather perplexed. Then she realized that he was probably joking and saw the funny side.

John, then went on to explain that he had informed his companions about his intended visit and had better return to them and inform them about the following proceedings. He then boarded his craft and flew it into the hastening gloom.

"Well, what did you think about that astounding visit, he seemed to be very genuine," said Alison.

Art then agreed that John seemed to be entirely genuine. Both continued to venture far and wide on their own planet of Terre. Yet again they encountered the weird and the wonderful. The creative design scientists had produced this beautiful bird with incredibly ornate plumage that glistened with gold purple and silver. It was of a prodigious size with an enormous wingspan. As it fluttered it's wings seemingly to build up momentum, it opened its gigantic beak and emitted a timid tweet. Both Art and Alison collapsed with laughter at this ludicrous event.

They spent many months continuing with the exploration of their fascinating world. They had just descended to a fertile plain and Art had made himself comfortable. He had just seated himself on the only boulder in the area when he broke the silence.

"Do you realise that although we have covered almost the complete extent of the planet, it's strange we haven't heard a thing from John? I hope that he is ok. He did tell us that many of his companions wished to exterminate us and didn't agree with them. Maybe, they took exception to his wishes and did away with him. But then, he is probably ok, he strikes me as a born survivor," said Art.

"I would guarantee that your comment is perfectly correct, and he is ok. However, there is one important subject that I would like to discuss with you. Do you envisage that we could procreate successfully? During our many excursions, I keep getting intense feelings for you" replied Alison.

"Well, peculiarly enough I have been suffering the same feelings for you. Taking this further, when we were both created, we were both manufactured containing the exact molecules within us. I have this insane desire to reproduce small species within us," said Art.

"Then how do we find out about this reproduction thing?" queried Alison.

"Yes, I agree that it will be a problem and will contain a major input of trial and error and of course a great deal of experimentation. However, I am sure that we will be able to work it out together and will have a great deal of fun finding out about copulation. By the way, when would you like to start?" questioned Art.

"Well, there is no time like the present" came the quick response.

Several days later, amidst laughter and pure joy, they were still hard at it. Both Art and Alison were amazing creatures and were hugely athletic. Then at last they pulled apart completely sated.

"That was extraordinary" was all Art could murmur.

However, they still hadn't heard anything and began to feel uneasy about the situation. Time seemed to fly by, and they still hadn't received any further communication.

"Do you comprehend what is happening to us? We are creatures of industry and are not conversant with wiling away our time. I would therefore suggest that we return to the area of huge towers that are encased in dazzling reflective materials and endeavour to seek the whereabouts of John," said Art.

Alison's response was immediate, and she agreed to journey with him. Then they both decided that it was far more expedient to travel the aerial route by sphere. It took no time at all for Art to manufacture the sphere and they hurtled in the direction of the city of dazzling towers. They landed their sphere inside the city on some ornately tiled artifact and decamped from the sphere. Art had discovered that one of the new powers that he had been endowed with was a homing device, that allowed him to establish contact telepathically, with the contact of his choice. A few moments later, he had made direct contact with John.

"I should have realized that I would be betrayed, there were too many factions working against me. They have imprisoned me in an area that is ten levels below the main street. It is well-nigh impregnable, and I feel that I will probably be locked in here forever," said John.

"Well, we have good news for you, John. You are about to be rescued," said Art.

One of the many powers that Art had been granted was the power to feel. This enabled him to feed on the emotions that were rising from many street levels below him. He thrust himself downwards until he encountered John's negative thoughts. Art then emerged in the small cell where John was imprisoned. Art then encased John in his perfectly manufactured sphere and hurtled upwards and finally emerged on the ornate artifact. Alison was waiting for them when they both finally emerged.

"Well, that was astonishing. I am still not certain what happened, one minute I was subterranean and then we hurtled into daylight and freedom," said John.

"Then, I really do think that we should do some forward planning. Your erstwhile friends will certainly be after you as soon as they discover that you have escaped" replied Art.

"With our increased powers, we should be able to flummox them completely. We should be able to construct so many false gateways for them to follow that it will probably blow their minds" continued Art.

"Yes, I agree totally with my lover's sentiments, we are both here to protect you," said Alison.

For the first time in ages, John felt a perpetual calm swoop over him as he realized the fervency in Alison's gaze was firmly locked onto him. This giant female creature instilled honesty in her gaze and the fear instilled by his previous imprisonment rapidly dissipated.

"Well, as they have located us on numerous occasions at this location, I suggest that we relocate ourselves to another venue. Perhaps in the purple mountains on the other side of the red sea. However, these are nasty dudes and attack is the best form of defense, as no doubt, being creatures of habit, they will probably return to the same area where they endeavoured to destroy us the previous time. When they land, I will have manufactured a minute gizmo that will record their intentions. In this way, we will be able to forestall any nasty surprises that they may wish to inflict on us" concluded Art.

"I must issue a word of warning concerning David, he is not to be trusted. Although, he was my previous travel companion and I thought that he was ok. When I returned to the centre having just visited both of you, he revealed his true colours and had me arrested, his reason being was that I had consorted with the enemy. In fact, if you hadn't rescued me, they would have left me to rot down there," said John.

"Yeah, he doesn't seem to be a very nice individual, could this be a trait of humankind?" demanded Alison.

"Well, humanity has its faults, just like many of the other races that are spread

throughout the galaxies. But the quest for power sometimes even annuls the quest for survival" commented John.

This revelation left them in yet another quandary, as they felt that their next move must be totally justified. This was because both Art and Alison had felt they must protect the earthlings from themselves and curtail any devious practices that they may commit.

Then as punctual as ever, six aircraft approached the previous landing site and launched a ferocious attack on the site. Art had foreseen that this would be a possibility and had rigged up a reflective mirror device that multiplied the spheres prodigiously. Then the occupants of the craft landed and had a cursory inspection of the remains of the spheres. Tattered pieces of crystal and a sticky substance were all that remained. The pilots then conferred and climbed back into their craft and flew off.

"Well, they were obviously not too observant. Left the listening device in plain view and they never spotted it" said Art.

"That was an interesting visit that they made. Somehow David appears to have made himself the supreme leader. I wonder how many more bodies he had to trample over on his meteoric rise to the top," said John.

"Yeah, he is the most obvious nasty one. However, as they conferred for quite a long time, it will be interesting to find out the salient points of their conversation," said Alison.

Art manhandled the listening device into position and switched it on to a loudspeaker. Immediately a voice projected itself loud and clear. It was the supreme leader David who had bestowed the mantel of leadership upon himself.

"It seems to me that we have very few options open to us, since these ungrateful creations that we created, have taken it upon themselves to rebel.

However, performing this act will lead to their complete obliteration. We have no other alternative but to destroy this planet and its noxious lifeform. We shall fly the mothership off the planet and bombard Terre into extinction" concluded David

Art gave a grim chuckle and then continued.

"They really have a problem with their long-term planning. They still don't realize how powerful both Alison and I have become. They will rue the day if they endeavour to bombard us into extinction," said Art.

There wasn't much more that they were able to do. It seemed that their only option was to play a waiting game. Then much to their consternation on the far horizon, the outline of the huge mothership appeared. John registered that neither Art nor Alison seemed perturbed in the slightest. However, the mothership seemed to be incurring difficulty in getting off the ground and was actually shuddering and trembling in mid-air. The mothership then descended rapidly and crashed into the ground.

"Oh dear, they seemed to have met with some kind of accident" was Art's callous response.

Alison regarded Art with pity but said nothing. In the meantime, John had rigged up a spy scope and seemed to be studying the crashed mothership intently. Although, the mothership had crashed over fifty miles away, John could pick up the details quite clearly.

"Well, it appears that my nemesis David has made it out of the wreckage. There seemed to be about two hundred of my former comrades that were intent on obliterating the planet Terre" complained John.

"Yes, I am afraid that neither Art nor myself could allow that to happen, hence the downing of the mothership," said Alison.

"That is absolutely incredible, you mean to tell me that both of you were instrumental in crashing the mothership? How would that be possible?" inquired John.

"There is a major problem in how humanity arrives at a solution to a problem. As a race, it concludes that everything should be clear-cut and straightforward. Both Alison and I have completely different concepts, possibly as we have just been created. Our new powers derive totally from our imagination. Therefore, if you think that something must happen, it always does," said Art.

"Now, be truthful you are informing me that purely by willing that the mothership should crash you inspired it to do so. Your new powers rely purely on autosuggestion. I find your explanation somewhat bizarre," said John

"Ok then you of little faith, there is really nothing else for me to do but to give you a demonstration of these powers. You can clearly see that lofty mountain over there that towers up into the sky, well it's not there, it is here. Sorry about that it almost crushed you" said Art.

"Well, that is a travesty of everything that we learned as humanity. You are informing me that just by believing that something may happen, it is certain to happen. However, don't perform another demonstration, after being nearly crushed by a mountain, I believe you," said John.

The three of them had discussed their varied options and had viewed Art's impressive demonstration. They decided to plan not only for their own future but also for the future of humanity. However, they still hadn't a clue how to rid themselves of David and his nasty accomplices. Then the decision was completely taken out of their hands as a ravening energy beam smote a purple boulder beside them.

"Well, I suppose that you would register that as a near miss. I am, however, becoming a trite fed up with these silly games that humanity seem to be indulging itself in" complained Art.

"Then what I propose that we accomplish, is a gesture of the total power at our command," said Alison.

"Your wish, is my command, my love," said a smiling Art.

The following instant, there was a flash, and they were transported to the area of dazzling towers. The wrecked mothership was still disgorging the passengers that had remained on board. One of the passengers, who was behaving in a strange manner, was David. He seemed to be rubbing his head frequently and was muttering incoherently.

Art strode over to the vicinity of the unpleasant man and endeavoured to communicate with him. This was without success as he kept repeating the same words. Alison had materialized at the same time as Art and strode over to converse with him.

"What did you discover about David and what was he saying to you?" demanded Alison.

"I am not too certain what he was saying, he kept on repeating that his head was hurting. Maybe he damaged himself when the mothership crashed" replied Art.

"The manner in which it seemed to be cavorting about, that is extremely likely" agreed Alison.

"Well, I don't think that David is going to be much of a challenge he seems to be away with the fairies," said Art.

"Yeah, well it seems that our main opposition to a quiet and peaceful life seems to have been eliminated" responded Alison.

Humankind had voyaged for many years in their FTL mothership to escape from the ravages that they had wrought on their own planet. Then having destroyed their own planet by bad management, they took it upon themselves to create other lifeforms on their mothership, having learned nothing from their previous experiences. They endeavoured to adopt the mantel of supreme beings and of all-powerful gods in their new environment. Unfortunately, for humanity, their scientists created another being that adapted instantly to the surroundings. Their telepathic communications contained both understanding and compassion, which were not the ingredients to be found in humanity's makeup.

The new lifeform that humanity had created was completely different and had no delusions of grandeur. However, they possessed incredible powers, that through imagination, could originate many things. These beings had really no concept of good and evil but as long as they felt comfortable with their decision, they would carry it through. Both Art and Alison had a loving relationship and begat many children. However, unlike humanity, they were wise and fair in all their decisions.

Therefore, if you possess a faster-than-light ship and require a new planet, I would most certainly recommend the planet Terre. Then if you encounter Art and Alison, give both my love and warm wishes.

Ad infinitum.

RATUS

He didn't realize who he was or indeed what he was. However, he knew for certain that he was, and existed. Did He have a brain? He must have, otherwise, where did that thought come from? He stretched himself out and something seemed to click inside him. He stared at the iridescent wall of the cave that contained him and a misty reflection formed itself in front of him. He had a long hairy snout. He instantly knew what it was because his mind told him so. As he was unable to estimate either his length or size, he remained in a quandary. This didn't last long as his mind informed him that he was gigantic There again he was on the horns of a dilemma, as he couldn't comprehend the meaning of the word. Just a few moments later the misty reflection on the wall gave him an idea of what the word gigantic entailed. Literally, thousands of creatures had appeared on the wall. However, when he compared himself to the other creatures, he was by far the largest. He rose to his full stature and smashed his head into the roof of the cave. Half stunned, he staggered into the blazing light that emanated at the entrance.

The heat was intense and became magnified by the burning rocks that encircled the cave. He retreated into the cave, to escape the burning rays of the scorching red orb that lurked in the sky above him.

The burning rocks that encircled the cave, also trapped the heat. Varied thoughts invaded his brain, which had fervently analysed his various options. He had searched the cave for any materials, that would aid his survival in this inhospitable place. Eventually, he was successful and found a strange material that he managed to pierce with a pointed object. Without knowing it, he had designed the first parasol on the planet. Under the cover of his new invention, he stepped out into the searing light of the boiling planet. Except it wasn't anymore, it was pitch black. It was as if somebody had turned the light switch off and extinguished the sun.

Ratus, which was the name that he had decided to call himself, was totally unperturbed. As he had discovered that he had excellent night vision. Something small and what he would call insignificant scurried in front of him, but he barely noticed it. Ratus strode onwards ratfully, until he slammed into a door. This had the immediate effect of stopping him dead in his tracks. He pushed the door gingerly, but it flew open with a crash. An enormous figure was seated at the table in front of him. An ingratiating smile was playing across his lips.

"Welcome, I am the god that can make all your desires, become a reality. You are a rat, admittedly a rather large specimen. As I have just consumed rather a large quantity of happy juice, I am feeling exceedingly beneficial to all and sundry. This of course includes you, my large rat friend. What do you desire?" Demanded the god.

This time Ratus became extremely perturbed. In one moment he had exited from the stygian darkness into the world of a huge green god who was prepared to grant all his wishes. Where was the catch? He was highly suspicious.

"You may not be aware but one of the advantages of being a god is that I have the power to read minds. In your case, it is quite an endeavour as you have only just been created and your mind is in a frantic turmoil. I can understand your incredulity at having any wish granted. Perhaps I am able to point you in the right direction? This planet is already teeming with life would you like to be the ruler and be King?" said the green god.

A look of amazement spread across the features of Ratus.

"I am not certain what my function would be, as I have never been a King before" queried Ratus.

"Well, my intention would be, to make it as easy as possible for you. I suggest that you should marry a Queen, In order to complete the picture" replied the Giant.

RATUS

"Where on this planet would I encounter a Queen? I am sure that we move in different spheres" said Ratus.

"There would be no problem about that I haven't created her as yet," said the smiling green god.

There was no doubt that Ratus had become even more perplexed. The green god had offered him the position of King on this newly created planet. Then to make the situation appear even more bizarre, he suggested that Ratus should be accompanied by a Queen. Then the green god smirkingly, informed Ratus, that he hadn't even created her as yet. Still dumbfounded he addressed the green god.

"Then when exactly do you intend to create this Queen of my dreams?" demanded Ratus.

"The answer to your question is self-evident" replied the green god.

Ratus span around, whilst following the green god's gaze, a tall and elegant figure was entering the god's chamber. In the eyes of Ratus, she was absolutely stunning. Her jawline was refined and her whiskers somehow moulded into her fine features. She halted in midstride and stared intently at Ratus. Then a thousand fireworks seemed to explode simultaneously into his brain. Then she smiled and he fell instantly in love.

"Well, there you are! And what do you think of your newly acquired Queen?" your majesty queried the god.

"From the first moment that I saw her I instantly fell in love. She is magnificent and totally adorable. By the way, I am conducting this conversation in an extremely loud voice in order that she can receive the gist of it" said Rufus.

"Yes, I certainly heard the myriad of compliments that you bestowed on me. So, thank you, as I am completely under deserving, as I have only just arrived here," said the Queen.

"Do you know something; I am really getting into this creating business. At the moment everything seems to be going as planned. Both of you seem to be getting along famously," said the smiling god.

The Queen languorously strolled over to where Ratus was standing. She then surveyed him up and down.

"Not bad for a genuine hunk of masculinity. I accept you as my love partner," said the Queen.

"Yes, then we both agree. We will endeavour to rule this planet as best we can" said Ratus.

However, the green god hadn't finished with his arrangements. Ratus and his lovely Queen were designated a large palace with an exotic garden. Numerous species volunteered to attend to their daily needs.

Then the coronation took place, and both the King and Queen were crowned with magnificent crowns. Diamonds, rubies, and sapphires adorned both crowns in great abundance. After the ceremony, a great feast had been prepared with vast quantities of food and wine on offer. Both joy and happiness were proffered to the guests and the celebrations continued until well into the morning.

The following day the newly crowned couple emerged from their chamber Both of them were somewhat worn, after a night of prolonged passion. As they were about to enter the lavish banqueting hall of the palace, the green God materialized in front of them.

"Don't worry about your servants, I am invisible to them. I have come to discuss your impending reign. By the way, did you enjoy your night of rumpy-pumpy?" demanded the green god.

Ratus completely ignored the furtive questioning of god and replied accordingly.

"Both my Queen and I have decided fairly and compassionately. Yes, we have heard rumours that a savage hoard of barbarians is intent on invading our kingdom, but we intend to stand firm. But, come to think of it, there is only one god involved in the creation and that happens to be you" said Ratus.

"Well, you are turning into a fast learner. I am guilty as charged. However, there was an ulterior motive behind my devious behaviour. I realized that you needed the challenge to progress your leadership. Hence, I created the barbarian hoard" explained the god.

"Then yes, you are a tricky devil. You have created a King and Queen to indulge your private passion for wargames," said the Queen.

"Yeah, you are not such a good guy after all. What happens when this nasty hoard arrives and slaughters us all? said Ratus.

"Oh, I wouldn't allow that, as soon as they got the upper hand I would smash them into smithereens," said the god.

"Well, that doesn't seem exactly fair either. I thought that when you created us you would grant us free will and we would be able to make our own decisions. Now it appears that you have turned yourself into some kind of control freak and we have no say in our destiny" complained Ratus.

Both King and Queen left the palace and meandered through the exotic gardens. Twisting and turning by a small river that winded its way through the fragrant gardens.

"Well, let's hope that he is not eavesdropping on us. To be honest I am not sure if I trust this god anymore. He seems to make up our destiny as we progress along. The problem is that he seems to be totally omnipotent and takes great delight in creating everything. But at least he created you for my perpetual enjoyment" said Ratus.

"In your dreams, lover boy. If you don't meet up with my high expectations, I will be away like the wind. I consider myself a free spirit and will not be held back by any restrictions," said the Queen.

"Well, I do like your determination, and I hope you succeed," said a nearby voice.

"Where, by the seven rings of our planet, did that voice come from?" demanded Ratus.

"It came from me," said the voice.

"Then you must be incredibly minute, I can't see you," said Ratus.

"Yes, you are correct in your assumption. If you glance to the right of where you are standing, there is a small bush, that bush is me," said the voice.

"This is most intriguing and must be a planet first. A talking bush" said Ratus.

"However, that is not all that I am able to do, watch this!" said the voice.

There was a flash and the ground beneath them seemed to tremor and a large fierce creature with razor-sharp teeth appeared in front of them. It roared in anger and yet seemed unable to move.

"I have rendered this creature immobile, and it will be unable to move until I allow it to do so," said the bush.

"This situation is becoming weirder and weirder and weirder. First, we had a talking bush. Now, it has gone a million steps further and it has obtained the power of creation," said the Queen.

"Well, at least the green god has some competition in the creation world and maybe the bush will be able to aid us," said Ratus.

"You keep on mentioning the green god, who is he?" interjected the bush.

That is an exceedingly pertinent question. The green god informed us that he is the lord of creation and that without him, our planet would be devoid of life and would have no beings" said the Queen.

That is the biggest heap of rubbish and the worst untruth that I have ever heard" said the bush.

Then it became extremely agitated and started to jump up and down. To make matters worse, the razor-toothed creature came to life and lunged forward. It stopped instantly at the bushes' command.

"Sorry about my temper but I became very frustrated when I heard your explanation of the green god's creation abilities. It is a very simple procedure to create anything. This is merely a case of mind over matter. You must employ your imagination to form an entity, and then observe the result," said the bush.

Then it appears that we have been completely misled by the green god and we may have the power to create locked within ourselves" said Ratus.

"That is a totally correct assumption, why don't you give it a try?" said the bush.

A determined expression appeared on the Queen's face, as she concentrated on the task ahead. There was a movement in the air followed by a loud pop and a beautiful fairy creature with gossamer wings materialized in front of the Queen. The problem was it was knee-high to a grasshopper and totally diminutive. Again, her brow furrowed, and the fairy vanished.

"Well, at least I managed to produce something, now you have a go!" demanded the Queen.

Ratus complied instantly and concentrated on producing an entity. However, much to the Queen's amusement nothing seemed to be transpiring. After about ten minutes, he went over to a section of the wall and clouted it with a large hammer that had appeared in his hand. It made not the slightest impression on the wall and seemed to bounce off it.

"What, are you playing at? Whatever it is, it seems a waste of time to me," said the Queen.

"Well, just how wrong can you be? I have been conducting an experiment to protect our palace and its surroundings from any attack that may occur from the green god. I have constructed an invisible barrier that will defy any attack launched by the green god" said Ratus.

"Then, it appears that you intend to tackle the green god head-on. I am still not sure of your reason, as he has provided everything that we have ever desired" responded the Queen.

"Yes, and there is a simple reply to your asinine comment. A short time ago we both agreed that we didn't trust him. Now, you seem to have changed your mind and taken the easy path to acceptance. However, he is as fickle as the wind and may decide that he has no use for us and destroy us. We have no freedom and are at the mercy of a mad god's whim" said Ratus.

"Do you know after your short but eloquent speech you have convinced me to change sides again? I will support you until my dying breath" said the Queen.

She went over to where Ratus was standing and engaged him in a lascivious kiss. In the meantime, the bush had materialized in the palace and had observed Rattus' demonstration.

"Superbly done, it will provide you with a great deal of protection. But the green god may launch his attack from another angle. Therefore, I suggest that you should indulge yourself in espionage. This must be your best option. In this venture, I am prepared to act as your spy. They will never suspect me I am just a jumble of atoms" said the bush.

"Well, thanks for the offer but it is far too, dangerous. If they were to catch you, he would totally disseminate you and your jumble of atoms would be annihilated" said Ratus.

"Do you know, you must be the bravest and most courageous bush on the planet, for such a small and insignificant creature I find it truly astounding" praised the Queen.

The days passed by and still no attack was launched by the green god, although ominously, it had been reported that hordes of savage barbarians were massing on their borders. As they were directly challenging the power of the green god, the fear was that he might even allow the barbarians to slaughter the previously protected King and Queen.

However, when the attack was delivered with a virulent message of rage and anger, as far as the green god was concerned, the barbarian attack was repulsed and thrown back into his face. Ratus had constructed the invisible forcefield barrier with immaculate precision and it had worked to perfection. Then the green god tried another gambit and encouraged his horde of barbarians to cross the river border and invade the kingdom. This turned out to be a complete catastrophe for the invading force. The people of the kingdom were defending their lives and their families. The royalist defenders had another advantage, one of their numbers had just invented the bow and arrow. Thus, when the horde of savage barbarians endeavoured to traverse the swiftly flowing river, they were met by flights of arrows and were cut down in their thousands. Most of the barbarians ended up shaking their fists at the sky. It was probably from the sky that the green god had given the barbarians the order to attack.

The royal couple had armed themselves and had ventured down to the river, where they discovered that their services were no longer required, and returned to the palace.

"Yeah well, the green fiend will be planning his next move. I should think that he was not overjoyed with the considerable pasting his troops had to endure. but I am certain that haven't heard the last of him as yet," said the Queen.

"Oh, the big guy must be totally disgruntled, especially after we defeated his invasion force," said Ratus.

Just as Ratus finished speaking, there was a flash and the bush materialized in front of them. The Queen was so surprised at his rapid entrance that she stepped back into an ornamental statue and brought it crashing to the ground.

"Sorry about that, but I didn't heed your words of warning and decided to involve myself in espionage. Incidentally, the green god isn't as bright as he thinks he is. He doesn't. even seem to have any security surrounding him. I was able to listen to how he intends to carry out his next move".

"Well, done, although I did fear for your safety. What did you learn from your spying activity?" demanded Ratus.

"That he is in the process of creating a vile and satanic creature. This being, will have some very unpleasant powers gifted to it. This includes the gift of poison and fire. The creature will be half serpent and half dragon," said the bush.

"You seem to have performed your spying activities rather well. Have you any thoughts on how we may destroy this mythical monster?" asked the Queen.

"Actually, I think that I probably have a solution to our problem. I think that the combination selected of serpent and dragon may have dire consequences for both curious combinations. Basically, the serpent is a lover of cold dark places of the underworld, whereas the dragon is a lover of heat and roaring hot temperatures. Therefore, I would surmise that as soon as this monster has been created, we should lure it into a massive volcano and see what happens," said the bush.

"Well, I fully understand your desire to lure the beast into a volcano, hoping that it will explode. What happens if it doesn't?" inquired Ratus.

"Then, I will apologise as I was totally wrong." replied the bush.

It was quite a few hours later before the mythical monster was created. When it was created and came into view, it was obvious that it was a poor creation by the green god. As it flew over them, it appeared lopsided and ungainly. Then to make matters worse, the bush had created a flock of flame birds, knowing that they were a dragon's favourite delicacy. Then the dragon, who was the major control partner in the ensemble, veered off in the direction of the flame birds. The volcano was also in the same direction that the flame birds were heading. Then it appeared that the serpent tried to take over the command of the body. Then, unfortunately for the combatants, the struggle became even more intense. The dragon belched out great spumes of fire. The serpent replied with poisonous fumes. Back and forth they lunged in contorted madness. Below them, firebombs were hurled at them, from the direction of the spluttering giant volcano. Then the wrestling match was over, as the dragon broke away from the serpent. However, in doing so he had dismembered the entire body. The remains of the serpent plummeted down into the crater, thumping down into a sea of lava. The dragon himself was totally unbalanced and followed the serpent down to meet a fiery death. Because of the makeup of the dragon of combustible material, when it hit the roaring flames of the volcano, it exploded with a massive blast. Shreds of the mythical monster were dispersed in all directions.

"Well, congratulations bush, your prophecy was extremely accurate, and we are the victors. Also, the creation of the flame birds was a stroke of genius. Without a doubt, you are a clever little bush," said the Queen.

"I concur entirely with my loved ones' comments, you have played the game cannily. However, we must beware of becoming too confident. No doubt the green god, will be hatching another strategy to catch us out" stressed Ratus.

"No, I am not hatching any further plots to eliminate you. I have no desire to continue this charade any further. You have passed my test with flying colours," said the green god.

RATUS

Then there was an almighty flash, and they were all comfortably seated in the royal palace. The bush was also one of the occupants of the chairs. The green god had also appeared and was as enormous as ever.

"When I created you all at the beginning, I was unsure of my powers. Then I undertook to establish by experimentation, the most deserving and trustworthy of my creations. Yes, I misled you on numerous occasions, particularly when I created the serpent dragon monster. I also threw many obstacles in your path, but you surmounted all with courage and fortitude. Who could have possibly envisaged you as King and Queen? Then ably supported by an extremely intelligent bush you went into Super Drive and transformed into the beings you are today. All of you have proved that you believe in freedom and honesty. With this in mind, I have no hesitation in bidding you all farewell and foraging far out into the galaxy. There may be other worlds that I can assist" then the green god vanished.

"Well, after all the ups and downs that we encountered it appears that the green god is a man of his word. He appears to have vanished into the wild blue yonder. We have been left the guardians of a planet that is teeming with creatures. What is our purpose in life, my Queen?" asked Ratus.

"Possibly to procreate and have little ones, I would guess. However, I am not too certain as I have never done it before" replied the Queen.

"Well, I have to admit that I am in the same boat as you, I haven't a clue how to make babies. However, I bet that we will have a lot of fun whilst finding out" replied Ratus.

In a distant galaxy, many light years from planet earth thrived a harmonious world ruled by a King and Queen. They begat many children who carried forward the dynastic aims of peace and prosperity. If you are lucky and arrive in your FTLS, you're faster than a light ship, you will find an enlightened land full of joy and happiness.

Ad infinitum.

A KENTISH CONSPIRACY

Quite a few years ago in a bygone age, there were three brothers of magnificent stature. Their names were Hengist, Horsa and Henrick. They were jutes and had invaded from the Netherlands. Luckily enough for the existing inhabitants, these jutes were of peaceful demeanour and had no interest in bullying tactics. Therefore, under the brothers' well-meaning tutelage, they prospered. Amazingly enough, in later years because of the brothers' love of all growing things, Kent became known as the garden of England. In certain parts of the world, slavery was rampant, this was not so in the domain of the brothers. They believed in sharing any produce including fruit amongst their workers.

However, all was not well in the land of Kent. An enormous threat had emerged from across the seas. Massive hordes of barbarians had gathered in fleets of ships and now threatened to invade the garden of England. Hearing of this alarming news, the brothers called for a council of war. The brothers, nevertheless, had one distinct advantage, the territory where they administered their benign rule, lay a couple of hundred miles from the sea. This would entail the barbarian horde facing a huge trek across many miles of open countryside.

However, unfortunately for the brothers, the leader of the barbarian horde was an evil man called Grim. He took extreme delight in rape and pillage. He originated from a vicious tribe called the Hun. Grim's one desire in his unpleasant life was fame and fortune. Therefore, to enable this to happen he would have to conquer Kent, the land of milk and honey. Grim had many slaves at his disposal and would use his ships to transport the vast amounts of treasure that he intended to amass. His idea was to equip the ships with rollers, and he would trundle his newly acquired booty across the fields and marshes of the countryside that he had invaded. The brothers not wishing to be caught unawares stationed lookouts on the coast to warn them of any impending invasion. Time flew by and there was still, no news about the whereabouts of the barbarian horde. When the first sightings were made of the horde, the Kent gardens were in full bloom with essences of honey being captured by the wind.

One of the coastal observers, having run for days, alerted the brothers to the danger that the barbarians had breached the coastal defences. Then, under the command of Grim, the slaves dismantled 200 of the boats and placed them on rollers. The trundling of these huge vessels across vast swaths of land was both arduous and extremely difficult. Grim had no time for shirkers and with cajoling and frequent use of the whip, he kept the convoy moving. Many of the slaves had perished on the way and still after a month of hard labour they were still only halfway there. The slaves were in open revolt against the treatment that they had been receiving. Grim put an end to their moaning, by having a number of them publicly strangled in front of their comrades. This was the final straw for one of the slaves and he set fire to one of the boats. This didn't help the plight of the slaves as Grim had the head of the slave lopped off. In the meantime, one of the slaves had escaped and made the brothers aware of the appalling conditions that his comrade had existed in.

Hengist decided that he had heard enough of the violent exploits of the evil Grim.

"Ok, we have a good idea of how this guy rules by terror and it will be only a few weeks before he arrives. My suggestion would be that instead of sitting on our buts and waiting for him to disappear, we should search him out and give him a good pasting. After all the best form of defence is attack" said Hengist.

There was no shortage of volunteers to attack Grim's column of barbarians and slaves. Hengist had decided that their best option was to attack the enemy column under cover of darkness when senses would be dulled.

Hengist, also ascertained that his own workers would have an incredible desire to protect the garden of England from this barbarian menace. It eventually took just over a week for the brothers' war party to encounter the horde. They could hear Grim's horde from miles away as they stumbled through the darkness guided by badly lit torches. There was no need for the brothers to advance any further, they would have to wait by the track to attack the horde. The incessant bad language and the rumbling of the rollers became louder and louder until the foremost boats rounded the corner. This was when Hengist and his brothers attacked the column. With a shuddering tempo, the column came to an abrupt halt. The barbarians were pushed backwards with the fierceness of the attack. The brothers asked for no quarter and gave no quarter. They attacked the horde wielding huge battle axes and cleaving to all sides of them. In the stygian darkness, there could only be one winner. The horde broke and fled. However, Grim was made of sterner material and didn't capitulate so easily. Besides this he had formulated another plan should anything go amiss. He grasped a large box that nestled under his feet and jerked it forward. Then he cried out.

"Release yourself into this world and bring pain and abomination".

Instantly, a mist transposed itself from the box and began to thicken and swirl around ominously. Grim through his evil thoughts and actions had unleashed upon the world the box of evil desires. Then a dreadful stench rose out of the box signifying both terminal illness and corruption. Then there was a vast explosion which hurled Grim backwards. Tendrils then emerged from the remains of the box and grew exponentially. They were blotched and mottled as if they were dying from an infectious disease. Grim frantically threw himself off the roller craft that he had been sitting in and landed heavily on the ground. The probing tendrils pursued him and Grim raced away in terror to escape the invasive horror.

The three brothers had viewed Grim's predicament from afar and watched as he was pursued by the vengeful tendrils. However, there was no escape for the evil Grim. Exhausted, he collapsed on the ground, but unfortunately for him, the tendrils hadn't been sated as yet. They were the contents of the box of evil desires. They attacked Grim from every single angle and entered every orifice in his body. Blood in vast quantities gushed out of his mouth. His buttocks clenched in agony as the tendrils found the correct openings. He screamed in agony as the box of evil desires struck hard into the centre of his nervous system.

Finally, Hengist, who was the oldest of the brothers exclaimed "Enough is enough. How much more will this punishment entail, I am going to end it."

Then he strode over to where the incoherent babbling Grim lay, his mighty axe firmly grasped in his hands. He wielded the axe far above Grim's head and sliced down. The blow completely severed the head which dropped to the ground. The cerebral cord was sliced through. However, as the head rolled along the ground, the eyes opened for an instant and a voice in his head said "thank you".

Hengist stepped back in amazement and stared at his brothers.

"Did you hear that?" he exclaimed.

Both acknowledged that they had and said that he was probably very grateful to be released from his torment.

ANTI CLIMAX

He was created on a planet known as Earth which had suffered a calamitous disaster. The previous prime occupants of the planet were called humans, who through science became incredibly technically advanced. However, humanity had a major flaw in its design. On repeated occasions, it refused to accept advice from its scientists on Global Warming. One of the main results was glaciers melting and sea levels rising. Included in this package of the disaster were cloud forests dying and wildlife under threat. Humanity had been one of the main instigators of Global Warming by utilizing gases to power their modern lives. Greenhouse gases as they have been so aptly named were now higher than they have been in the past 800,000 years. Climate change is also caused by certain gases in the earth's atmosphere being enabled to trap heat. These gases allow light in but keep heat from escaping. Therefore, they are called greenhouse gases. Following this catastrophe because of the melting ice caps, the sea level rose dramatically, and the world's weather systems became totally unpredictable. Earth's atmosphere which is known as air, is layers of gases retained by earth's gravity and had protected all life on earth. Then literally from 2020 over the following 50 years humankind destroyed their protective atmosphere by not heeding the advice of their scientists. Many of the oxygen-giving resources had completely been eliminated and the atmosphere of the planet had been altered. It had now reversed one of its previous effects and wiped out almost all lifeforms on the planet. This included the techno-wizardry that had enabled incarnations and had become almost entirely nitrogen based. This had been a gift to mankind. On the other hand, the ant fraternity not only survived the cataclysm but prospered across the globe. Formerly when humankind had been the main driver, the ants had not been gifted with any kind of intelligence, although they were able to communicate with each other through chemical signals. Before climate change there existed over ten thousand species of ants across the globe. Amazingly enough, as the Formicidae were the only major lifeform on the planet, they too had been gifted with intelligence.

Since climate change, Gozo's physicality had changed dramatically, he was now a significant figure of over a meter in length. The Queen, whom Gozo had never encountered, had the main purpose in life was to produce thousands of eggs so the colony would survive. There are wingless females, whose sole purpose is to forage for the Queen and protect the community. They never reproduce but are forced into a never-ending life of drudgery. Like so many other things in Gozo's busy life, he had no idea where on earth he had been created. Like so many of his species, he had been born into The Amazon Rainforest. Ants are enthusiastically social insects and lived in structured communities. At one time, there were also unusual species such as the yellow crazy ant, whose one desire was to build super colonies. Unfortunately for them, they were unable to adjust to the newly created earth's atmosphere and they all died out.

Gozo was not aware of one of the reasons for atmosphere change was humankind's burning and demolition of the rainforest. It was then that Tan the light of his life entered his burrow. The world around him seemed to burst into song and time stood still. Tan was a brood ant and was not beholden to the Queen and thus able to bear her own tiny ants. Gozo expelled his chemical odour of greeting and then telepathically bid her welcome. Her response was immediate, and a fragrant aroma of flowers filled his senses. Gozo had no idea what a flower was, but he still was able to ingest its visual beauty.

Above them in the scorched and burnt remains of the forest, only insects survived in the 200-degree heat that burned down from above them. The planet earth's atmosphere had turned almost toxic with the radical change in its consistency. A telepathic thought entered Gozo's head.

"What do you intend to do with the rest of your life? Do you intend to remain here, wasting your life away?" said Tan.

"Do you know, I have been thinking about this for an incredibly long time. My choice would be to venture into the world outside in search of adventure. However, I would only be genuinely happy if you were to come with me" replied Gozo.

Tan gladly accepted his invitation and they set off on their magical journey.

A few days later as they journeyed onwards, a vast forest loomed into view. They entered the forest and headed for the largest clump of trees.

There was an intricate labyrinth of passages spread under the routes of a massive Sumaumeira tree. Previously before the atmospheric change, this was the largest tree in the rainforest and over two hundred feet tall. It had also been a haven for wildlife and protected them in its canopy from many of the lurking predators below.

At last, Gozo managed to force his way through the root system and entered the strange, forested area that lay before him. There was an intricate labyrinth of passages spread under the roots of a massive tree. He managed to force his way through the root system and entered a bizarre new world that lay before him. Tan was following him closely and almost collided with him when he stopped so abruptly.

"This is the most foul and dreadful stench that I have ever encountered, is this going to be our brave new world?" said Gozo.

Tan had also reacted dramatically as the stench hit her antennae.

"It smells of death, although I am not too certain what death is, as I have never encountered it before" replied Tan.

A vast clearing opened, seemingly for infinity, as a glimmer of eerie subliminal light pervaded the clearing. They both trundled onwards, Gozo still leading the way, until they emerged into an area of shifting mist that rippled to the far horizon. The mist cleared and they found themselves in an enclosure. There appeared to be huge bunches of mysterious fruit hanging from the upper branches. They both intuitively knew from the pheromones they received, that they were edible.

"Wait here, I am going up" commanded Gozo.

For a meter-long ant, Gozo was supremely athletic. By utilizing his enormous jaws and strong legs he literally ran up the tree.

He did consider himself to be an accomplished artist and had in the past, designed numerous leaf designs, for his lady love Tan.

Having chopped through the branches he hurled the fruit onto the ground where his lady love was waiting. He then dropped back down on the ground dragging huge bunches of fruit behind him. Then having seated himself beside her and they tucked into the bounty that lay in front of them.

Tan then sent a telepathic message to the male of her dreams. "This is fantastically amazing, and I am fit to burst. I don't believe that I can squeeze any more inside me," said Tan.

"I wonder what type of sustenance they were. Although the pheromones informed us that they were ok to eat," said Tan.

"I don't think that it really matters, but it was a thousand times tastier than the usual rubbish that the workers feed us on" said Gozo.

They left the orchard of forbidden delights and continued their adventure. The mist was dissipating and as it cleared, they realized that the ground they were traversing was covered with stunted trees that seemed to have been blasted into minutiae by some powerful force. Then rising in front of them was a mountain of vivid colours reds, oranges and purples glared down upon them. Both sensed a perfumed nectar that enveloped their antennae. They instantly were aware that the mountain that had risen in front of them was an enormous source of food. Both stopped in their tracks to gaze in wonder at this magical food source. However, the next instant they picked up a loud droning sound emanating from the magic mountain. Then an enormous hairy insect appeared from nowhere followed by a procession of five others.

Both Tan and Gozo remained routed to the spot not knowing what to make of this spontaneous apparition. What they both did not realise was that like themselves these other insects had grown to enormous proportions because of the atmospheric change and were bumblebees. Just like ants they were social insects and were ruled by a Queen. Unlike army ants who are omnivorous, the bumblebees only dined on nectar. These big, winged behemoths buzzed with a frantic intensity yet offered no threat. Gozo and Tan observed the comings and goings of these monstrous creatures without realising they were completely harmless.

After a few minutes of studying these amazing creatures, Gozo sent a telepathic message to Tan saying it was time to move on. They departed from the magical mountain. Then almost immediately encountered a huge stretch of water surrounded by marshy ground. They decided to remain on the lakeside bank and travel as far as the trees they could see in the distance. As they approached, they could see a great deal of fluttering taking place in one of the trees. A display of blinding crimson lit up the sky. There were three birds, again all of them were of prodigious size. The two males were obviously fighting over the right to mate with the female. Feathers flew in all directions until one of the scarlet Macaws flew off, having submitted to his adversary. Both the lovesick ants had sheltered under one of the sprawling trees and were hidden from the conflict. Although they were each a meter long, they considered themselves diminutive, as opposed to the aerial combatants. They slunk away from their shelter not wishing to give notice of their movements. They were free to wander where they wished to go without any incumbencies to hold them back. They made their way along the lakeside until it became dark, and they decided to stay until daylight returned. Although they both had incredible night vision and were able to react instantly to any sudden movement, they had no experience of the land they were in and therefore decided to move cautiously. They still had some of the strange fruit with them left over from Gozo's acrobatic endeavours. They dined and replenished their energy levels.

It seemed to be almost immediate, that the dawn broke with a resounding crash. They both leapt up in unison and decided to follow the lakeside path.

"We are going to need some kind of sustenance before too long, but we also have to be very aware of any nasty predators we may encounter," said Gozo.

"I agree with you entirely my lover, especially having viewed the size of the creatures surrounding us "replied Tan.

They heard strange growling noises in the far distance. Their vision was impaired by the thickening mist that swirled around them. Indistinct mutterings and weird cries continued to follow them wherever they ventured. They also had the uneasy feeling that they were being constantly watched wherever they went. Then the sky above them cleared dramatically and in the far distance, they heard a loud boom. The wind whipped up to a gusting frenzy and the sky turned an ominous shade of black. In the meantime, the star-crossed lovers hurried for cover to escape the impending deluge. Then there was a huge crack of thunder which was followed by torrential rain. This was the commencement of a highly charged electrical storm. Forked and sheet lightning sizzled their way across the sky. Just in front of them, a bolt of forked lightning struck a tree with a terrific thump and the tree exploded in a great gout of fire. This had the effect of instantly illuminating the previously darkened forest around them. Zig zag of lightning continued to invade every area of the sky, interspersed with the crash of thunder to provide musical backing. Three more trees were subjected to the lightning, not wishing to dampen the ardour of the light show they blazed up into the black sky accordingly. Although they had been subjected to torrential rain, the wind had picked up and was fanning the roaring flames. The forest alongside of them had obtained a graveyard silence and both felt they were no longer being watched. The rain continued to sluice down, but the forest fire remained in charge. There was a sudden thrashing about in the undergrowth beside them but that died out and nothing emerged. With the roaring inferno within the forest both Gozo and Tan decided that it was time to make a move. It was still pouring down with rain, but they thought it was a much better option than being roasted alive. They were moving along the lakeside at speed, sustenance forgotten and fear driving them on. Yet again a jagged fork of lightning speared the tree in front of them and they came to an abrupt halt. Then it exploded into a huge ball of fire, and they knew that there was no way

ANTI CLIMAX

forward. Telepathic communications flashed in between them to formulate a plan.

"Perhaps we should go into the forest, the area ahead is just a mass of conflagration and there is absolutely no way through" postulated Gozo.

"I have no problem with that, the lightning seems to have not had the same effect in the forest interior" replied Tan.

They found that to both of their amazement as they entered the forest, the pathway was clear of any obstacles. It also brought them around the blaze-aerial combatants. They slunk away from their shelter not wishing to be involved in a mass conflagration and carried on into the forest.

"There is absolutely no way through" postulated Gozo.

"I have no problem with the lightening. It seems to have not had the same effect in the forest interior" replied Tan.

The inferno had pushed them along the lakeside again. The mist had cleared, and they could see into the far distance. Far across the lake, they could just make out a couple of large winged bright blue insects that seemed to be skimming low over the lake, which were most probably dragonflies, inherited from the human period. As they approached a large cluster of trees, they could hear a distinct buzzing sound. They also noticed pendulous sacks of something that these large bees seemed to be attracted to.

"What are they doing they seem to be a smaller version of those insects that we previously encountered?" Queried Tan.

Gozo wandered over until he was positioned exactly under one of the sacks, which conveniently dripped some kind of substance as he got there. He crouched down and surveyed the substance with his antenna.

"This seems to be extraordinary stuff and will be incredibly nourishing. It has the effect of acting like liquid dynamite. It has the power to convert itself into a never-ending source of energy. I think that I may be able to hook a couple down with this long stick, which will let you indulge yourself in this superfood and keep you going forever" said Gozo.

He then proceeded to unhook numerous sacks from the branches of the trees, and they all came crashing down. Amazingly, the sacks were strong enough to contain the incredibly viscous fluid within. Gozo then dragged the heavy sacks over to a huge log where they were able to feast on the food bomb at their leisure. The buzzy insects did not seem at all bothered about the thievery that had taken place of all their hard work. Having digested the delightful sticky substance and being totally sated, they both reclined on the log in a somnolent contented state. Tan nuzzled up to Gozo, he had gained her trust and love thousand times over. Neither of them wanted to be the first to move as they lay there in perfect contentment. However, eventually, it became time to move on. Gozo rose to his full stature and grabbed the sacks of untold nourishment and was on his way. He also realised that something strange had begun to happen to him. Whereas in the past he had been content to crawl, now he found that he was now so well balanced that he was able to stand erect on his rear limbs. Tan had witnessed his new ability with admiration and managed to emulate his actions with total success. The two of them strode on in perfect unity both in body and mind. They had reached another stretch of marshy ground when they came to a shuddering halt. Reclining on a decaying log was an enormous insect staring at them through malevolent eyes. Gozo tried to contact the creature through his newfound ability of telepathy. There was no response. This creature, whatever it was, was displaying the most enormous sting that culminated with a huge spike on the end. With its hateful eyes still locked on to the two lovers, a tremor quivered through his wings, as though he was preparing to take off. Gozo began to search anxiously around, for something to defend themselves against this evil entity. He had already dropped the sacks of the wonder food, when he spotted a long-pointed piece of wood lying idly on the ground. The insect was striped with bright yellow and black, which seemed to signal 'don't come too near, I am dangerous'. Gozo then grabbed the long-pointed lance and thrust it in front of him to deter the incoming attacker. The yellow-striped attacker began to weave frantically about to confuse the holder of the waving lance. However, in the mind of the defender, he had right on his side and a

ANTI CLIMAX

loved one to save. The hornet speared its way downwards at an impossible speed, its huge sting thrust out in front of its targets, there would be no mercy shown.

Gozo was standing erect on his hind limbs. At the last moment, he swayed gracefully to one side and stabbed his lance upwards at his incoming nemesis. The force of the hornet's downward descent was instrumental in his own destruction. The steadily held lance impaled the hornet with one vigorous movement. Then a dying wave of anger washed over the hero Gozo. Tan rushed over to where he was standing, the still-dripping lance drenched with the innards of the hornet.

Tan sidled over to where the hero was standing and yet again nuzzled up to her loved one.

"Oh, my lover and saviour I offer myself to you for eternity and all that I desire from you is hundreds of little baby ants," said Tan.

Gozo smiled happily to himself and thought that there would be no problem with that. He just adored baby ants.

This is an interplanetary warning to any prospective inhabitants of planet earth. Pay attention to your scientists or lose your planet

Ad infinitum.

JIGSAW LAND

Span had appeared as if from nowhere. How had he arrived there? He hadn't a clue. This was possibly the craziest place that he had ever visited. As far as he could see the landscape was totally jagged and sliced into vast portions. There seemed to be no symmetry in any of the sections and Span became totally flummoxed by the whole situation. Then a voice emerged from the ether.

"Span, you are an innocent in the world of puzzles. However, as I am the lord of creation, I feel that it is my destiny to guide you through the many pitfalls that you will encounter," said the voice.

Span assessed his options which were few and far between and guided his thoughts in the direction of where he thought the voice must be and curtly accepted, as it must be better to be guided by something that knew the lay of the land. He mounted over the fractured landscape; the stark unevenness made it unforgiving.

"You have entered the periphery of Jigsaw land and my intention is to guide you through it and all the dangers that it entails" boomed out the voice.

The next instant there was a large crash and Span felt himself falling through the ground.

"Sorry about that I should have warned you. It is a fracture in the Jigsaw" said the voice.

"What by the seven moons of strontium are you talking about?" replied Span.

"Well, I suppose I should have informed you in the first place about the planets that I created, there are four of them and they are all game planets. The one that you appeared on is the Jigsaw planet. Then we have the Crossword planet and the Chess planet. Finally, I created the Card planet. All these planets are ruled by a queen called Chance. Then if you have lady luck on your side, you may become an all-time winner. However, in the meantime, I will give you a lesson on the power of your mind. Relax and I will convey you there" explained the voice.

Span did exactly as instructed and felt the voice intruding into his mind. Instantaneously he was transported through space and hovered over a planet that resembled a jigsaw. Majestic mountains towered into the sky and vast rivers surged through the ravines of the fractured landscape. Beyond the mighty cliffs that encased the ravaged land, raged angry oceans that pummelled the tormented planet.

"By the way, you were correct in your observation, that this planet is the Jigsaw planet and the planets far beyond it are its sibling rivals "informed the voice.

"Yes, it's very satisfying to be correct some of the time. But am I going to be stuck on this planet in perpetuity?" Demanded Span.

"Well, that is totally up to you, but first of all you must solve the problem of the Jigsaw planet by fitting the correct sections together," said the voice.

Span was just about to reply when he found himself hovering above the planet Jigsaw. However, this time the planet was endowed with extremely different features. Huge numbers had appeared on the landmasses which were numerically positioned. Span realised that the voice was guiding him to make the correct selection. Then working through the numbers from 1 to 20, he slid all the sections together. He achieved this incredible feat by using the power of his mind.

"That was exceedingly well done, and you are beginning to realise what a powerful tool your mind is. However, your journey has just begun and from there on the tasks become harder," said the voice.

"Hold on a minute, I am not in the slightest interested in playing your silly games. I don't know how I became involved in the first place" complained Span.

"Unfortunately, you are already deeply involved, and I can't possibly let you renegue on your promise" sneered the voice.

"What promise? I never made any promises to you" replied Span.

"I beg to differ when you accepted my offer to show you around. You made a verbal unbreakable contract with me which I intend to insist that you comply with" said the voice.

"Well, that is a surprise, I had no idea that people can be bullied into doing something without even signing a contract" complained Span.

"Anyway, you may not realise it as yet, but we will have a great deal of fun together and it will be part of your destiny" stated the voice.

"Well, as you have put it so eloquently, I seem to have no choice. Where are we off to next?" said a suffering Span.

"You have much to learn and your impatience is quite irksome. However, the next planet that we shall be visiting is the Crossword planet. Where you will have yet another problem to solve" said the voice.

"Then how long is this problem-solving going to continue? "Asked a fearful Span.

"When you have solved the problems of the other three planets" snapped back the quick rejoinder from the voice.

"Then it may take a lifetime to find the correct answers" complained Span.

"That is not at all likely, a trillion light years from the planets that I created was a planet called Earth, which unfortunately refused to accept advice from its scientists. This was something called global warming. Eventually, global warming happened, and all life forms ceased to exist. However, the most popular game on the planet was wordle, which had gripped all nations. Your latest task is to discover the answer to the question. What killed me?" Boomed out the voice.

Span realised that he seemed to be hovering above another planet. The change in landscape was totally dramatic, the harsh terrain of the Jigsaw planet had been replaced by rolling meadows and gently flowing streams.

"Let me introduce you to the Crossword planet, it is lovely and without a doubt my favourite planet," said the voice.

"Yeah, I agree with your judgement, it is delightful and by the way, I have solved your riddle and there is absolutely no point in going down there" replied smirking Span.

"Ok, then what is the answer to 'what killed me?" Said a hesitant voice.

"Well, you gave me a huge clue when you informed me about planet Earth. I reckon that the crossword planet is an exact replica of regions of planet Earth. Therefore, the answer to your question, 'what killed me?' Must be global warming" replied Span.

"Well, you are the clever one, you are correct. Just as well you were right, as I forgot to tell you that if you failed in any of the tasks that I set you, I would have to exterminate you" said the voice.

"This seems to be getting weirder and weirder. One minute you are my strongest ally and in your next breath, you threaten me with extinction. I realise that you are the omnipotent god of creation, but can't we go back to our former working relationship it will be much easier" replied Span.

"Fair enough, as long as you succeed in your task, I will issue no more threats. Now, let's revert to the planet that we are located on which is the Card planet. I have shuffled the pack, so it is no longer the final planet in my universe, it has been replaced by the Chess planet" boomed out the voice.

"I understand your reshuffling of the planets and therefore I presume that our minds are hovering over the Card planet?" questioned Span.

"Intelligence seems to be on the up with you, my friend. Therefore, my question is a numerical one. In the old languages of Earth, there was a language known as French. My clue is '21 that floats' and is in the French language and if you manage to solve this one, we will progress to the chess planet" roared out the voice.

Span, thought about the clue that he had been given and was a trite miffed at being unable to come up with an answer. So, it was a number in an ancient language that didn't exist anymore. Span had a natural affinity with numbers, and he started jiggling them around. Suddenly, as he continued to do so, a number shouted out at him. It was number twenty-one. He carefully analysed the number and it seemed to wish to tell him something. Something that floats was also part of the riddle. His mind then seemed to direct him to another ancient language, English, that no longer existed. Then the answer to the riddle hit him like a thunderbolt. There was an ancient card game called vingt et un, which when translated was twenty-one. Then there was also in the riddle '21 that floats'. In old English the same game was called pontoon, hence the floating connection.

"Well, what a roundabout route, but at least you got there in the end. I suppose congratulations are in order, so well done! However, as you seem to be rattling through my agenda at a hurricane rate, your next performance will take place on the Chess planet. I wish you luck" said the voice.

"Does he really mean it or is it just his way of admitting defeat in his stupid games?" thought Span.

Span realised that he better get on with the task of investigating the Chess planet. However, when he arrived there, he seemed to have arrived in the middle of a pitched battle. Two vast armies were sprawled across the landscape. They were attacking each other with a mixture of formidable weapons. Both armies were distinguishable from each other, by the colour of their armour, either white or black. Some of the troops were mounted on mighty steeds, that dwarfed the poor foot soldiers that were fighting alongside them. Strangely enough, there were also numerous religious men who were donned in bishops' outfits who were smiting their opponents with mighty blows from their croziers. Span realised that he was witnessing a battle enacted between humanoid chess pieces. However, the largest figures of all were the king and queen of the white army. Both of them were moving with speed and grace and appeared totally at ease with the situation. Although Span had no idea where their opposite numbers in black were located, the battle had obviously been extremely ferocious as their bloody armour would testify.

"I have a peculiar feeling about this scenario. Those white royalty must be up to no good and are planning something. By the way, my riddle to you is to be a winner, 'you must avoid moving or you will perish," said the voice.

Span cast his mind back to the frenzy of the battlefield and was dismayed by what he observed. Havoc and mayhem seemed to be the predominant players of the day. Then on the far reaches of the battlefield, the white royals were joined by a mythical creature a fire-breathing dragon. Span didn't know the rules of the chess contest but, had a fair idea that the white royals were cheating. Just as if to prove his point the dragon blew out a great cloud of flame which incinerated the defenceless black pawns in front of it.

"That is simply outrageous, I am going to intervene," said the voice.

"Well, are you allowed to do that? You don't intend to let this battle run its course?" replied Span.

"No, I have no intention to let this battle continue. Besides which I can't abide cheats. In these worlds I am the lord of creation and omnipotent, I make the laws and can change them" replied the voice.

"Then you probably have an enormous problem. If you are able to change all the laws of creation, you must always be correct. Therefore, in my mind, you have established a very unfair precedent, which is a form of cheating. Further to this and just to enhance your misery I have solved the riddle of the Chess planet, 'to be a winner you must avoid moving or perish'. The answer must be checkmate, which is the end of a chess game" stated Span.

"Well, you have been blessed with supreme intelligence and you are correct as usual. However, we still have the matter of the white royals to deal with and their infernal dragon" complained the voice.

"This is a very unusual situation in which you find yourself. Yet do you support one side or the other? Be they either white personified by evil or black which represents purity in spirit. You created this game planet and therefore are entitled to make any decision that you wish. However, I do advise that you make sensible choices otherwise you may set the Chess planet out of kilter" replied Span.

Unfortunately, the omnipotent being suffered from delusions of grandeur and didn't heed Span's advisory warning. The voice descended like a pestilent cloud and smote the white royals and their dragon with dire consequences.

There was a gigantic flash and a thunderous roar, and the complete contingent disappeared. The continuing disaster didn't stop there. Both the black and the remains of the white army collapsed in disarray. Then a stupendous gravitational pull clasped all the game planets in its mighty grasp and what had previously been created became uncreated. The four enormous planets that harboured many types of exotic lifeforms became punched out of existence. Span still existed for a short time longer. Then as he was expiring, he heard a pitiful voice in the far distance bemoaning his fate.

"I should have taken Span's advice. I had everything and lost everything. It's just terrible luck" faded out the voice.

Ad infinitum.

FLOWER POWER

She existed yet was completely unaware of where she came from. Her whole world consisted of a riot of colour the name that she had decided to call herself was Fleur. Then this gigantic plant exploded with a display of a thousand different flowers. The intense aroma that wafted over Fleur, was a combination of honey and fragrant flowers. It was then that a voice entered her mind.

"You have performed exceptionally well Fleur. However, it is now time to undertake a journey of adventure and wonder".

Previously, she had relaxed into a spiritual world of joy and contemplation. She dreamed of many diverse things but knew that her soubriquet was a flower. She had drifted through the clouds and the mists of her imagination until at last she finally arrived at the garden of her dreams. It was there that she planted the precious seed that she had nurtured so carefully. It was then that she witnessed an incredible sight. The small seed that she had planted burst out of the ground with explosive force. It then climbed rapidly to the tower above Fleur.

"This is part of your great adventure," said the voice.

Fleur then wondered what her next move should be. This was decided for her as her mind seemed to be embedded in that of a five-hundred-foot monstrous plant. Fleur strode forward and with one gigantic stride, she covered a vast stretch of ground and yet again the voice entered her mind. However, this time the voice issued strict instructions.

"You must forge onwards with your prodigious strides until you reach the emerald- green sea. This is an ocean of distinctive emerald, green water. Thereafter continue along the coastline until you reach the black swamp which will be many leagues away. This is where you may meet your nemesis," said the voice.

"This sounds rather scary to me. In what form does this nemesis appear?" questioned Fleur.

"The creature that you will encounter is the most hideous beast. It has the baleful stare of a serpent and takes pleasure in burning its victims alive with its fiery breath" replied the voice.

"Then, how do you think that this nightmare creature will compete with a five-hundred-foot plant that doesn't believe in taking a backwards step," said Fleur.

"You have a point; you are extremely large. I suppose that I will have to wait and see, "said the voice.

After this brief debate, Fleur continued her journey down the coast until she reached the emerald-green sea. The ocean seemed to be blazing with mysterious lights that hovered just below the surface. She carried on with her quest for many leagues and day turned into night on several occasions. Fleur had no problem with energy levels, as the baking sun seemed to renew her energy levels constantly. Fleur was certain that the mysterious voice was still somehow monitoring her. As night-time approached the emerald-green sea began to glow with a fierce intensity, guiding her ever onwards. Then daytime arrived again accompanied by the ravening sun. Eventually, the emerald-green sea departed to be replaced by a sinister black swamp. Then a raven black bird flapped into view and landed on the barrier that separated the path from the swamp. It then made a croaking sound as if to warn her of something that lay ahead of her.

"You know that it would be very advisable to heed his warning of the dreadful danger that you will encounter should you continue down the path that leads to the swamp," said the voice.

"Oh, it's you again I wondered when you would make another appearance, did you miss me?" said Fleur.

"No, I certainly did not, and I find your comment totally objectionable, you are inferring that I am spying on you," said the voice.

"Well, you must admit that since I started this voyage of discovery you have been popping up all over the place" replied Fleur.

"Yes, that is possibly true, but I have always had your best interests at heart," said the voice.

"Yeah, and I respect that, but I have found your behaviour to be most invasive" Fleur replied.

"Then I have to warn you, that your moment of truth is approaching fast and is in fact just around the corner," said the voice.

"I am in a blue funk and cringing with terror. Bring on my personal nemesis so I can shrink away from it in abject terror," said Fleur.

Fleur, then preened herself and rose to her full stature. She then concentrated her energy on visualising abundant flowers. Then rising up her gigantic stem, she bloomed into a thousand different colours. Intense perfumes pervaded the area attracting beautiful butterflies. Fleur simply oozed out sensory odours that heightened the senses and cast aside inhibitions. She then felt ready to combat her personal nemesis whatever it should be. Fleur then girded her loins and headed into the black swamp. A swirling mist that ebbed and flowed impaired her vision. She strode onwards eager to confront the creature that threatened her. Then having waded through yet another stinking mass of the pervading swamp, the mist cleared and she saw the abomination. The creature was exactly as the voice had described. Its body was that of an enormous serpent. Then it swivelled its head and transfixed Fleur with its baleful gaze. Fleur felt a surge of animosity erupting from the serpent. Then to complete the picture of intense hostility, it opened its jaws wide and spat a stream of fire at Fleur. Although she didn't realize it, Fleur's defences immediately sprang into action. The stream of fire that was heading directly at Fleur, seemed to hit an invisible wall and died instantly. The giant serpent spat another stream of fire at Fleur, but it had the same effect.

"Well, this is interesting, what kind of creature are you that can resist the fire of the serpent god?" Spat out the malevolent serpent.

"Yeah, well you do seem to have a huge problem you seem to have narcissistic tendencies that create an image far above your stature" replied Fleur.

"Ah, then you think that it is purely an image problem that I have and how do you suggest that I can remedy the situation?" demanded the serpent.

"Well, you do have an irascible demeanour and with your horrific appearance, you really need to improve your image. However, I think that I may have a colleague that may be able to help you" said Fleur.

The following instant, the voice who had been eavesdropping on the current situation, made his presence known by invading the minds of Fleur and the serpent.

"Well, I shall certainly endeavour to improve your image, snake, although we may have a huge problem. Unfortunately, in the past, you incinerated many of your victims. This didn't leave a very favourable impression with many of their relatives, relatively speaking," said the voice.

"Yes, in reply to your comments I take extreme umbrage at your asinine comment. I am not a snake I am a serpent" replied the serpent.

"Look, as far as I am concerned my major task is to improve your image. This can't possibly entail any visualization as your visage is quite horrific" complained the voice.

In the meantime, Fleur had retreated from the area of the monster and relaxed into a state of calmness and relaxation. Then having achieved nirvana, the multi-coloured flowers that adorned her, gave forth the most incredible fragrance. Her enormous stem was bowing under the weight of the blooms that were hanging off her. Fleur had literally turned into a blaze of glory. She was so stunning that the serpent caught sight of her and instantly communicated with the voice.

"Was this what you meant by improving my image? If so, I will climb on board, and you can represent me," said the serpent.

Fleur was amazed at how everything seemed to have turned around in the time of a few seconds. Suddenly images seemed to have jumped into the foreground. Obviously, the despicable and horrendous creature had totally reneged on his previous existence and now sought fame and glory. Still, at least she had another option open to her. However, she would have to be extremely careful not to let the mind-reading voice be aware of her intentions. She entered the swamp and casually approached the serpent. Then at the last moment, she stamped down hard on the foul beast.

There really was no competition, when five-hundred-foot plant stamps down hard on a three-foot midget there can only be one winner.

Ad infinitum.

ATMOSPHERE

He hadn't a clue of what he really was, or what he consisted of. All that he knew was that he seemed to be everywhere. Not only that, but a tiny proportion of him seemed to envelop everything. However, he had begun to realise that he was composed of many different elements, which was even more confusing. One of the elements that he was comprised of was something known as gas, which has no fixed shape. Atmos, for that was the name that he had decided to call himself, was able to configure himself into many extraordinary shapes. Atmos had also realised that he was also expanding himself over a huge landmass, known as a planet. He didn't even know if he was a male or something known as a female and didn't really care. However, he did feel that he was male. He also knew that he was essential in providing a safe atmosphere for the planet. This service that he would offer, allowed various life forms to prosper on the planet. Atmos, was driven by his need to find many solutions to obstacles, that may impede his progress.

As time flew onward at an incredible rate, he realised that he seemed to be getting more powerful and was forced into making decisive decisions. He reckoned that a combination of hydrogen and oxygen would provide a stepping stone to reaching a stable future for his planet. Yes, he had begun to think of this planet as his own possession. The major thing that bothered him, was the factor of a huge red object that burned incessantly in the sky, above his planet. Yet, although he felt the heat from its burning rays, as time passed, he came to accept it. As time roared on, he tried experimenting with numerous chemical combinations in his atmosphere. One of his experiments turned into a complete disaster. Atmos, had decided to introduce something called sulphur into the atmosphere. It was bright yellow in colour and when it fell to the ground it scorched the earth to the bedrock. He then decided to abandon his experimentation and carry on with his successful experiment of oxygen and hydrogen. He also discovered that an important by-product was something called water.

Atmos, through his inventive intelligence, also discovered that to keep the atmosphere routed to the planet, he would have to procure gravity. This turned out to be the hardest task that he had accomplished. It necessitated spinning the whole planet on its own axis. This he managed to do without flinging any objects from the planet into outer space. Yes, he had achieved his ultimate desire and produced gravity. There was also a hollow core to his planet which he decided to fill with volcanic material. This had the immediate effect of gigantic volcanoes being formed spewing out red-hot magma. As Atmos became more adept at constructing his planet, he imagined massive plates spread across the entire planet. He then jammed the plates together using impossible force. This had the effect of pushing huge mountains vertically upwards to soar into the sky. Without realizing it, he had terraformed the whole planet.

Atmos knew that his mighty task was only half finished. He had to find inhabitants for his newly created planet. Again, he had to experiment to find the perfect occupants. He rapidly discovered that oxygen seemed to be the most successful abundant element, to be utilized in the makeup of the occupants. Water consisting of two hydrogen atoms bonded to one oxygen atom also was effective. Having then studied the situation carefully, he began to create. His first efforts were absolutely dreadful, and he decided to try again. Atmos's problem was that he had never created anything before. Hence, he had not the slightest concept of the difference between beauty and grotesque. He laboured for thousands of years, to perfect his ideal inhabitants. On his lengthy journey, he began to become supremely confident in achieving a satisfactory result. Eventually, Atmos produced the being that he considered would be the perfect inhabitant of his planet. He also investigated the amazing discovery, that there were two sexes, male and female. On analysis, he further discovered that they were able to replicate themselves and produce smaller beings. Atmos had also decided, that he would also perfect a reliable atmosphere, to enable his new charges to breathe.

Atmos, then made a decision to leave his new creations behind and venture far and wide. He left the atmosphere behind him and sped on his way. His intention was to leave his planet behind and see how they multiplied. In a few thousand years' time, he would return and hoped to find a thriving community. His mode of travel was totally unique as he had created his own atmosphere. Initially, because of his planet's rotation, he was able to launch himself into space. In order to find his way back, he had adjusted a loadstone on his world. This would guide him safely back to his planet. However, that was only conjecture, as it would be many years in the distant future. In the meantime, many problems could possibly occur.

Atmos, foraged far and wide in his never-ending quest amongst the outer regions of the galaxies. Eventually, after three thousand years, having experienced the wonders of the outer limits, he decided that it was time to journey back to the planet that he had been instrumental in creating. Because of his positioning of the loadstone, he was able to journey back with pinpoint accuracy. Atmos, had decided to approach his planet extremely carefully as he didn't wish to alarm the creatures on the planet of his arrival.

As he peered down from his private atmosphere, he realized that his planet was teeming with life. There had been a population explosion which in certain cases seemed to have produced a negative result.. Atmos, in his limited experience of creating, had manufactured a bellicose being, with little love for peace and harmony. Down below him were thousands of the beings that he had created, indulging in hand-to-hand combat. Although their weapons were of a primitive nature, they were still causing bloody carnage. Backwards and forwards these militants thrust against each other, seemingly with spears and swords their only weapons. Atmos, was horrified at the scenes taking place below him. This was war at its most barbaric, with no quarter asked. Atmos was completely nonplussed about his next move. He was after all the lord of creation and could turn himself into the lord of destruction. Or on the other hand, he could just wait for the final result of the battle.

Then, yet another terrible thought struck Atmos. When he had first created these beings, there had been only two of them. Now, with the intensive breeding patterns that they had perfected, there were literally thousands of them.

The alarming idea that had just invaded his thoughts was that when he had created these savage beings on his planet, he hadn't estimated how quickly they would breed. The planet was vast and therefore highly probable that these bellicose beings, were carrying out their warlike activities on the other side of the planet.

With this scary scenario in mind, Atmos propelled his personal atmosphere to the other side of the planet.

It only took an instant and they had arrived on the other side of the planet, much to Atmos's horror. When he got there, the warring factions were behaving in much the same manner and seemed intent on battering each other to death. Atmos, was beginning to feel outraged by the antics of his created inhabitants. He really only had two options open to him. Firstly, destroy the inhabitants. Secondly, to start again and create entirely new inhabitants of the planet. Having mulled over his options and rejecting both of them, he decided to invent a third option. He would communicate directly with them and decide if he would destroy them or not. He then manoeuvred himself back to the other side of the planet, where he had first witnessed the savage behaviour of its inhabitants. Atmos, had noted that one of the attacking forces, seemed to be much better organized than the other. It was commanded by two members of the opposite sex, who had adorned their heads with strange headgear. Atmos, had decided that he had wasted so much time messing around, that it was better to take more direct action. With this in mind, he sent his personal atmosphere down, to apprehend the beings with the strange headgear. The transfer was instantaneous, and the creatures were deposited on the floor of the atmosphere. From his viewing platform, Atmos could see that both creatures were well-proportioned.

"What happened and where are we Queenie?" Questioned the man with a crown on his head.

"Yes, it's totally bizarre, one moment we were in the middle of a pitched battle and the following instant we were transported to this misty chamber," said Queenie.

"Well, so nice to meet you both" boomed out a disembodied voice. "Although, we have not had a formal introduction, my name is Atmos".

"Good to meet you, wherever you are. You seem to be a rather misty character. By the way, my name is Kingie" replied the male.

"Both of you are wondering why you are here and why I have spirited you away. The reason is that I created both of you and I have to make a decision whether because of your warlike aggressive behaviour, I should destroy your race or let all of you continue down the path of destruction" said Atmos.

Kingie's reply was immediate.

"What do we have to do to allay our destruction?" replied Kingie.

"Unfortunately, everybody is seeking to better themselves by whatever possible means. This quite often leads to a land grab, where land and property are seized" interjected Queenie.

The misty atmosphere started to swirl around rapidly and then stopped.

"Do you know you have explained the problem with your planet succinctly? Everyone is aiming to procure something that is not theirs. This instils in the inhabitants, the vices of greed and envy. You have both earned your redemption by explaining this factor. My decision is that I will spare your planet. However, my intention is to return to this planet in three thousand years to witness your planet's development. The unfortunate timing involved in this event is because of your limited life span, you won't be here to greet me" stated Atmos.

True to his word Atmos, bided his time and made plans to return to the planet that he considered his own. On his travels around the galaxies, he witnessed some terrifying sights. Including two red stars that seemed intent on smashing each other into fragments. He even journeyed into a black hole as he had heard on the grapevine, that he would emerge in a parallel universe. This was totally untrue, although on his return journey titanic forces endeavoured to crush him into a minimalistic effigy of himself. However, Atmos was totally unaffected by all the events that were in the process of happening as he had been involved in the creation of his own planet. On his way back he did observe a cataclysmic collision, between two gigantic planets, that seemed to have annihilated each other. Therefore, after such an exacting journey, it was a relief to emerge successfully above his planet. Yet again he had been guided to his destination by his faithful loadstone.

Atmos, hovered above his planet, visualizing huge tracts across his vast domain. What he had noticed almost immediately, was instead of the timbered habitation encountered on his past visit, magnificent structures now soared up into the sky and dominated the area around these buildings.

In the centre of this city was a vast square that contained enormous palaces. Numerous statues were positioned around the square, much to the amusement of Atmos, as he surveyed the statuary, he realised that two of the statues depicted Kingie and Queenie. On reflection, he remembered saying that when he returned, because of their short life span, they wouldn't be there to greet him. How wrong he was, as the two effigies were there to greet him. He had also surmised, from the other statues, that they had produced a royal bloodline, perhaps even continuing to the current day. Atmos carried on with his investigation around the planet. However, although there were sizeable towns scattered across the planet, there was nothing to compare with the grandeur or size of the magnificent city that he had first visited. Then having clarified that factor, he thrust himself back in the direction of the royal city. As he arrived, the midday sun was glaring down on the beautiful marble buildings. The reflection from the marble, dazzled Atmos, although shrouded in his personal atmosphere it had little effect on him.

He had decided that he would introduce himself to the current rulers of the planet. However, he must remain wary of any introduction that would present him as a godlike figure. There would be no fanfare of trumpets or banging of drums. When he introduced himself, it would be low-key. No flashes of lightning or thunderstorms. Through his snooping around in his personal atmosphere, he was already conversant about who the current King and Queen were. Amazingly enough, both were almost the exact image, of Kingie and Queenie, that he had encountered all those years ago. Atmos intended to be very surreptitious in his approach to the royal couple. Eventually, when they were alone and away from their numerous courtiers, he made his move. The misty atmosphere drifted into the royal couple's vision.

"You won't know me, but I am the creator of your planet and everything that thrives within it" boomed out the disembodied voice of Atmos.

"How, completely wrong you are. You are the stuff of legends, and your existence has been passed down throughout the ages. Before anything existed, there was Atmos" said the King.

"Well, this must be a ground-breaking encounter. I hadn't realised that I created such a stir when I met your ancestors all those years ago. This fame is most unexpected, as I always tried to keep a low profile. It now appears that I have failed dismally," said Atmos.

"I shouldn't blame yourself, you are regarded in most circles of our society, as the ultimate hero" replied the King.

"Well, that's very encouraging to know, as I have always tried to avoid the limelight" replied Atmos.

"Then, I would think that you would be quite interested to know the history of our dynasty. You arrived on the planet that you had previously created and made a vivid impression on our forebears. This enlightened them so much that they downed their weapons and concentrated on making a better world. Beautiful architecture burst onto the scene. Palaces and fortresses were built and agriculture flourished. The people were happy and content. Then raiders came down from the north intent on rape and pillage, our ancestors fought them off and sent them home with bloody noses.

"Then, a thousand years ago, just when everything was going swimmingly, horror struck our race and people began to die in droves. Plague of the most virulent variety, attacked on all sides. Coughing out great volumes of blood was one of the symptoms. Their bodies were blotched with purple spots. Some experienced such high temperatures that they exploded into flames. Others developed fits of shaking and often choked themselves to death. Eventually, the pestilence was over and everyone was free to bury their dead. Churches and temples sprung up across our lands including false prophets and sinister messiahs. However, we survived and continued on with our lives" said the King.

"The most important object that you gifted our ancestors, was the knowledge stone, "said the Queen.

"Yes, I remember it well. I manipulated the atoms in a massive strand. This enabled it to dive deep into the inner core of the planet and feed pertinent information on the health of the planet" replied Atmos.

"We treated the knowledge stone with the utmost respect and had teams of scientists constantly monitoring the results. If there were any sinister readings, we endeavoured to remedy the situation" said the King.

"Highly commendable" was Atmos's instant response.

Three hundred billion, light years away from this planet, was a similar planet known as earth. This was populated by a variety of humanoids of similar appearance to those created by Atmos. Unfortunately, the earthlings completely ignored the advice given to them by their scientists. This was a warning given on global warming. The surface of the planet heated up to such an extent that huge ice fields started melting. Oceans rose to stupendous heights flooding enormous tracts of land. Then the planet became even hotter and vast unstoppable fires devoured the planet. The atmosphere on the planet began to change rapidly and carbon dioxide became the main beneficiary. Because of the toxic atmosphere humanity expired in huge swaths. Every living lifeform ceased to exist, leaving a barren and inhospitable world.

Meanwhile, back on the world that Atmos created, all life thrived, under the burning red sun of an alien planet. Scientists were still monitoring the health of the planet on a daily basis. Art and culture were thriving, and the population were well fed. Peace and harmony prevailed and warlike actions were frowned upon. Should you be fortunate enough, to encounter this world on your travels, the inhabitants of this planet will greet you and make you truly welcome.

    Ad Infinitum.

CONDOR

The mountains surrounded him as he took off and plummeted down into the void. Then he opened his wings and began to glide across the frozen valley. Situated on all sides of him were the enormous mountains that soared up to perpendicular heights and blocked out any view of the early morning rising sun. He had been reared in the mountains in a dramatically perched nest. The other chicks in the nest had all perished before learning to fly. He had a bald white head, which thrust itself out of striking jet-black plumage. Yes, although he was part of the vulture family, he was not a scavenger, he was a predator. He also possessed the power of intelligence and had decided that he needed a defining name. His thoughts were in such a discombobulated state that after much cogitation, he decided to call himself Rodoc. He leveled out his flight path and drifted on the wind. He was intent on searching for his favourite prey, the mouselet, a small but delicious rodent. He spotted one of the small red animals almost immediately and swooped down to make his kill. Unfortunately, he missed his target and was left grasping at a pile of dust. Then disgusted with his inept performance, he flew back into the mountains and alighted on a lofty peak.

"Well, you are a magnificent creature, I would think that you must be a condor," said a voice.

Rodoc was completely nonplussed at the comment, as he hadn't been aware of any other avian nearby. When eventually the avian intruded into his vision, he was simply astounded. Seated on a boulder a few feet from him was one of the most stunning avians that he had ever seen. Rodoc, knew instantly that it was a mythical creature, a Starbird. This avian seemed to shimmer with a thousand different hues, blues, reds, and purples briefly shimmered to be replaced by another different colour. The shifting display was both dazzling and memorable. The Starbird had incredibly long plumage that was streaked with silver and gold.

"Thank you for the compliment, but in comparison to you I am dowdy and uncolourful and lack the blaze of beauty that you provide" replied Rodoc.

The Starbird studied Rodoc for several minutes and seemed to be digesting his inner thoughts before replying.

"If you follow me, I will take you on a journey of excitement and everlasting joy," said the Starbird.

With an invitation like that Rodoc found it hard to resist and their magical journey began.

The planet that Rodoc had been created on, was thousands of lightyears away from planet Earth. This was a planet that had ignored the advice of their scientists and was stripped of its atmosphere and denuded of all life. A cataclysmic ending that was hard to ignore.

Yet, on Rodoc's planet, microdust and various gases had formed in the atmosphere and created the planet's genetics of life.

Rodoc was in hot pursuit of the Starbird as he hurtled through a narrow gorge, when there was a blinding flash and he seemed to have been transported into a totally different area. On all sides of him rose huge ice mountains. The Starbird had come to a slithering stop. Whilst in front of her was stationed an enormous white figure. Rodoc, knew instinctively, that the creature that he was observing was the mythical snow leopard.

"I would like you to meet an old and very dear friend of mine. He is called Cuddles" said the Starbird.

"Well, what a very strange name to call him. He doesn't seem very cuddly to me" said Rodoc.

"Yes, I expected some weird comment, issuing from a bald minute flying chicken, such as you," said the Snow leopard.

"Now boys, behave yourselves. There is absolutely no need to insult each other. I am sure that when you get to know each other you will get along famously" demanded the Starbird.

"Well, he started it by casting aspersions on my name. I do like to be loved by everyone and I apologise, but what kind of flying chicken are you?" demanded a smirking snow leopard.

"It seems to me that your apology is fraught with insolence. For your edification I am a condor" replied Rodoc.

"Both of you are really behaving like infants, you should grow up both of you" advised the Starbird.

Rodoc decided that he would be the peacemaker and set about building bridges between himself and the feisty snow leopard. However, the snow leopard was truly gigantic and was at least over a hundred feet tall. Rodoc launched a sudden assault on the enormous snow leopard and flew directly at him. The snow leopard was routed to the spot and Rodoc landed on his head, much to the consternation of the snow leopard. Then the condor with two flaps of his mighty wings landed on the back of the snow leopard. He then inserted both mighty claws and gently massaged the back of the snow leopard. This seemed to have an immediate effect on the mighty animal who issued a low purr of perfect contentment. Then the sound seemed to get louder and louder culminating in the roar of a mighty engine.

"Thank you. You have earned my eternal friendship. I have never experienced such extreme pleasure in my entire lifetime" purred the snow leopard.

"Well, that wasn't too difficult, was it? Now it's up to you both to look after each other in perpetuity" said the Starbird.

"We will" they both chimed in together.

Then ok, as you are both the best of buddies, it's time to bid Cuddles farewell and we will be on our way" said the Starbird.

A short time later, Rodoc and the Starbird, were flying down the ice-strewn gorge and as they flew, they conversed.

"Yes, I was certainly very apprehensive the moment that I met Cuddles. However, everything seemed to work out after I gave him that massage. I would suggest that his real problem must be loneliness. Unfortunately, he is unable to fly and is stuck in a freezing valley with no way out. Well, oh beau-

CONDOR

tiful tour adviser where are we heading next?" questioned Rodoc.

"Well, I would like to introduce you to another acquaintance of mine. However, we do have a fair distance to cover and as opposed to the freezing climate we have been forced to endure, we will be heading for a red-hot climate" replied the Starbird.

"Then, I have to congratulate you on being such an incredible tourist adviser. You promised me excitement and adventure, which has already come to pass. Now we are venturing into another area of the world, which has extremely hot temperatures" said Rodoc.

They had stopped their journey for the moment and were resting on top of a small hillock.

"Well, that countryside that we have just passed over was truly amazing. Masses of vegetation seem to be springing up all over the place, as we progress to warmer climes" said Rodoc.

"Yes, your assumption is spot on, but we have still a major part of our journey to complete, and it will get even hotter. There is hardly ever any rain in the region that we are heading for, and it is quite arid" replied the Starbird.

Then, having rested and having briefly conversed, they set off from the hillock and into the unknown. They flew on for many hours. The landscape that they encountered, varied dramatically on several occasions. They flew over roaring torrents of water and stupendous waterfalls, then above forests with lofty trees. As the climate warmed still further, they encountered jungles. However, there seemed to be very little life. They advanced even further, the temperatures rose, and the land became more arid. Eventually, the land seemed to have developed into a desert and was incredibly stifling.

"We have arrived at our destination. I suggest that we should descend here, and I will search for my acquaintance" said the Starbird.

Rodoc, hastily agreed that she should search for her acquaintance and then wondered apprehensively, what she would turn up with. However, when she eventually turned up his worries disappeared immediately.

"I would like you to meet a very dear friend of mine, his name is Tachee.

He is a cheetah" said the Starbird.

The reason for Rodoc's current demeanour was the creature in front of him was a beautifully spotted animal with graceful lines and obviously built for speed. However, he was unable to stop himself from thinking 'Oh no not another feline'.

Immediately a thought entered his brain.

"So, you have already met Cuddles, have you? He is enormous and quite scary. Whereas I am far smaller and infinitely more friendly. Although I am able to run faster than you can fly" boasted Tachee.

"That is probably not true. I will race you some time and the winner can take all" replied Rodoc.

"Fair enough and if she is agreeable, we shall employ the lovely Starbird as the adjudicator" said Tachee.

"No, I am not agreeable to be a participant in such a trivial contest. The planet that we inhabit needs our constant attention otherwise we may all perish. We are aware of a malevolent force gathering strength on the high mountains and it is our duty to combat such evil" replied the Starbird.

"Well, where exactly are these high mountains so we can route out this evil and who are these creatures?" Questioned Rodoc

"We believe that these creatures have only just been created, but already they have an incredible aura of menace around them. We will have to journey back to the high mountains where we first had our blissful encounter. Situated to the rear of those mountains is a vast volcano and that is where these creatures' intent on conquest have gathered" replied the Starbird.

"Then you are informing me, that close to the ice mountains where we first met, there is a huge volcano which no doubt is spewing forth intense heat. Then why hasn't the ice mountains melted and disappeared completely?" demanded Rodoc.

"Yeah, that is probably because our planet has only just been formed. However, from the effects of the volcano, a vast lake has already been created.

"OK, now we have just learned of the seriousness of the situation. What do you suggest should be our next move? Asked Rodoc.

"Well, including Cuddles, there are only four of us and we are going to be hopelessly outnumbered. There again Tachee cannot fly" said Starbird.

"Don't worry about Tachee, I am large enough to transport him myself unless he has a fear of heights" said Rodoc.

No sooner had he said that Tachee with a massive bound landed perfectly on Rodoc's back between his wings. Then Rodoc soared up into the sky, whilst Tachee screamed with delight at the novel experience. Unlike the previous journey, there was no stopping on small hillocks, they were on a mission. Their voyage was fast and furious and totally unabating. Led by Starbird they flew towards the setting sun so rapidly, that the sun was unable to set.

"Cuddles is forcing his way through the ice mountains and should arrive at the volcano in a couple of hours" the airborne Starbird informed her companions.

"Yes, I wouldn't like to be in the shoes of this menace when he arrives," said Rodoc.

They glided down onto the plain in front of them. Tachee leapt off his avian steed and raced up and down with incredible speed. A vast lake spread out before them and in the far distance the enormous volcano soared up into the sky. It was belching out fire and brimstone. Rodoc flapped his enormous wings and strutted up a down to maintain his equilibrium. The Starbird shimmered her feathers and they commenced glowing with an unearthly hue.

"These invaders are continuing to emit an aura of menace but peculiarly I can't distinguish what they actually are. There may be some kind of forcefield blocking my probe" said the Starbird.

"I shouldn't worry excessively about that, just keep on probing. Far more worrying is where Cuddles has got to, he should be here by now" said Rodoc.

"Well, he did have a long way to journey, and he is a very lonely fellow. Therefore, it is quite likely that he is communing with an intelligent rock" replied the Star bird.

"An intelligent rock I have never heard of such a thing. Do they exist?" Questioned Rodoc.

"Only in the mind of Cuddles, he is such a solitary fellow" replied the Starbird.

Just then, there was a loud holler and Cuddles came striding around the corner. He seemed to have gained a new lease of life and a zest for living. Rodoc, then explained about the evil entities and how they were located near the volcano. Rodoc explained that he and all his companions must cross the lake to get to the volcano, and immediately Cuddles understood the problem.

"Then we need some kind of craft to traverse the water. This really should be quite easy to do, as our avian friends will be able to take the aerial route. I intend to lop down a few trees, to build a craft sufficient to contain Tachee and myself" explained Cuddles.

For the next few hours, the four of them laboured incessantly, to complete the task before them. Cuddles was so immensely strong that on several occasions, he snapped huge trees in half with his bare hands. Eventually, the craft was built and launched. However, it was an exceedingly strange shape in order to accommodate Cuddle's huge bulk. Tachee was manning the improvised oars but the progress across the lake was painfully slow. Both Rodoc and the Star bird were flying alongside to give them encouragement. Finally, they obtained their objective and arrived at the far shore. Poor Tachee, was totally exhausted and collapsed in a sodden heap.

"Well, we have arrived at our destination and to prove it we are here. What is the plan from now on?" said an exuberant Cuddles.

The silence seemed to be everlasting, as the four companions remained silent. Not thinking a word.

"The situation that we have found ourselves in, is quite complicated. As the Starbird is unable to ascertain what exactly is the physiology of these creatures, although she says that they are continuing to exude considerable menace. Therefore, our best option must be that we continue to the volcano, to find out what exactly we are dealing with. I would also suggest that although

Starbird and I are flyers, we should not range too far ahead of you but remain as a team" requested Rodoc.

Tachee had completely recovered from his ordeal and bounded up the steep incline that was baring his way to the volcano. Matching the huge striding Cuddles, by utilizing his superior speed. As agreed, both Rodoc and the Starbird literally, hovered above the earth-bound duo on their way to the volcano. There was still a long distance to cover before they reached the foot of the volcano. They were all informed on a regular basis by the Starbird that they were heading in the correct direction to the enmity that was being broadcast. They had just rounded a bend at the foot of the volcano, when a giant slither bug jaws agape, rushed straight at them. Tachee jumped adroitly aside, whilst Cuddles stamped down hard on him. The result being, one entirely splattered slither bug. The volcano seemed to be getting more and more bad-tempered and was incessantly rumbling and grumbling away. To make matters worse, it had started to spew out fire and death in the form of molten lava. All four of them began to worry that there would be a gigantic eruption. Starbird then informed that the threat from the menace that she had located was situated near the summit of the volcano and had risen dramatically.

"OK guys, this is becoming ridiculous. I am going up to the summit to find out what exactly we are up against" said Rodoc.

He then flew off, intent on reaching the summit of the volcano. An hour later he returned to report on his findings. They gathered around him to listen.

"Well, there is absolutely no point in going to the summit of the volcano, because this threat has ceased to exist. Yes, when I arrived at the summit there seemed to be a great deal of friction in the air. I descended onto the volcano carefully just in case I was going to be the subject of an attack. It was then that I spotted these creatures that had been giving off this aura of menace. They were incredible, tiny minute insects most probably ants. I trod on one of them just to be sure that it was sentient, and it screamed in agony" reported Rodoc.

"In that case, this planet will no longer require our services. Unless of course, we are inflicted by some nameless horror from another galaxy. However, my next question must be, who amongst them will take on the title of guardian of this planet? As I appear to be doing all the talking, I have a suggestion to make. Both Rodoc and the Starbird would make admirable guardians, therefore as Tachee is nodding his head, maybe he is falling asleep. The motion is carried" said Cuddles.

In a distant galaxy far far away, a guardian had been chosen. If when your FLS carries you there in search of adventure, don't tarry too long or you may get stamped on.

AD Infinitum.

BOGWIT

She didn't know exactly what type of species she was, the others around her informed her that she was a Bogwit. In the first place, it was really quite mystifying how she had arrived on the planet. One moment she was somewhere else and then she had materialised. The others that she had conversed with, had materialised at exactly the same time. The problem she had, was that she had to find something with a reflective surface, to view herself. There were ten others in her group. She was not a numerist, but the number ten seemed to have popped into her head. There was a pool of something in front of her, maybe it would be able to act as her reflective surface. They were all dressed in something that was called fur. They had big ears and inserted into their mouths were white sharp pointed things that were called teeth. Oh, and by the way, she knew she was a female because she felt like one. She also realised that she was a giant of a female as her head rose into the canopy of something called a tree. She wondered if those around her had named themselves. She had decided that a naming ceremony was most important. Therefore, she decided to name herself Marshwiz. It sounded far better than Bogwit. She then informed the other Bogwits about her naming ceremony. Pandemonium broke out as they began to scream out names at each other. Eventually, Marshwiz had had enough, and she stormed off into the trees. However, she was closely followed by another Bogwit that followed her into the forest.

"Hello, I apologise for intruding in your privacy, especially as I haven't had the courage yet to give myself a name. By the way, I am a male and you are a stunning female" said the Bogwit.

"Well, thank you for the compliment. I must say it's not every day that I receive such gracious comments. I will now endeavour to choose a suitable name for such a delightful being as yourself. Yes, you are smaller than I and masked by the trees you have a certain aroma I shall name you Chiplet" said Marshwiz.

In the distance, they could hear that the other group of Bogwits, were approaching their communication hideout rapidly.

"Not that I have anything against the incoming traffic, but I think that I have developed a penchant for an adventure with you," said Marshwiz.

"Well, we are encroaching into what appears to be a massive forest. I am certain that none of the other Bogwits will dare to follow us into the stygian darkness" said Chiplet.

Both of them decided, that the best way to make their escape from the approaching multitude, was to venture deep into the forest. Then having decided on their course of action they strode off into the forest. They had barely brushed past the first few trees when Chiplet voiced his concerns to Marshwiz.

"Do you know where you are going?" Chiplet postulated.

A voice boomed out from the tree ahead of them.

"Do you, know where you are going?" the voice demanded.

Chiplet glanced at the tree that was situated straight ahead of him and spotted a large purple bird that was sitting on the lower branch of a tree. Marshwiz had decided that being somewhat larger, she was the senior adviser in the partnership. She then fired off a vitriolic broadside at the purple bird.

"You may think that you are exceedingly clever by your acidic repetition However, when I reach you, I will rip all your feathers off and teach you a short sharp lesson" replied an irate Marshwiz.

"You may think that you are exceedingly clever" sneered the purple bird.

By this time Chiplet had rushed to Marshwiz with an explanation of the purple bird's rudeness.

"That purple bird sitting on the tree over there probably means no harm. Unfortunately, he is a mimic and is repeating verbatim, every word that you say" said Chiplet.

"You really must think that I am stupid, I grasped the situation immediately. He is performing like a parrot and repeats everything "replied Marshwiz.

Authors note. This was a bizarre comment as parrots were a totally unknown species on original worlds. However, I suppose that I should allow some sort of artistic license.

Not at all flummoxed in any way, Chiplet strode on through the forest and passed under the tree where the purple bird resided. The bird surveyed him as Chiplet passed underneath him but said nothing. Marshwiz had caught him up and apologised to him.

"I am so sorry, I can't comprehend what came over me and what in the heavens is a parrot?" said Marshwitz.

"That is perfectly ok, I wasn't offended in the slightest. I suggest that we carry on with our journey, wherever that may be?" said Chiplet.

Marshwiz overtook Chiplet and lead the way. The trees had begun to thin out considerably when they exited the forest. Ahead of them was grassland that led to yet another vast outcrop of rock on which was a substantial cluster of trees. With Marshwiz leading they both made considerable progress and rapidly arrived at the outcrop. However, the cluster of trees was most deceptive, as they entered a forest that was far denser, than the forest from which they had just exited. Marshwiz was no respecter of leaf or needle and smashed her way through any impending blockage. Chiplet followed in her wake, thankful for her bulldozing tactics. Both of them had just rounded a massive tree, when a stentorian voice rang out forbidding them to trespass any further.

"Where in the demonic shades of Bogwit, has that voice come from?" questioned a perplexed Chiplet.

"I am down here you oversized moron, your powers of observation are as untrustworthy as your mind," said the voice.

"He is a mini creature, with an incredibly rude mouth, he is situated by your right foot. Don't, tread on him" requested Marshwiz.

Chiplet then glanced down to his right foot and spotted the minute creature instantly. To state that he was minute, was a perfidious understatement. He was absolutely miniscule but with an incredibly loud voice.

"If you don't mind me saying so you don't seem to have a strong bargaining position. You are as minute as a dust mite but tell me are there any more weeny people like yourself?" demanded Chiplet.

"Yes, there are thousands such as me, be very scared as we do seek terrible revenge against unbelievers" said the miniscule.

"Wow, what a scary being you are and now you are threatening that we will be exterminated by hordes of your comrades," said Marshwiz.

It was at this moment that there was an interruption from the tirade being launched by the miniscule.

"Don't believe a word that this idiot is telling you, he is an inveterate liar and to put your mind at rest there are only the two of us. We have not a clue how we arrived here. We both metamorphosed at the same instant. By the way, I am seated on a branch over your head "said the miniscule.

"Then, you must be very agile to climb up there" said Marshwiz.

"Not really we have wings, and I flew up here."

"That's very interesting" said Marshwiz.

"You seem far more eloquent than your brash companion, "said Chiplet.

"Well, the problem with him is that he has delusions of grandeur and feels that everyone should be subservient to him," said the second miniscule.

"That is completely outrageous and unfair. I have supreme confidence in myself because I am never wrong. Whereas my dithering companion is unable to make any decision and procrastinates forever" said the first miniscule.

"Yeah, well we can carry on discussing your predicament forever. However, the major factor in the scenario must be, that you are both incredibly small, whereas we are towering giants. If we wished to, with one step, we could crush you both into a faint smudge" said Chiplet.

"Not me you couldn't, I am still seated on the branch over your head, but with regards to my bombastic companion you are very welcome to obliterate him. He is a nasty bit of work with an inflated ego" said the second minuscule.

"OK, enough is enough and I am quite sure that we are both totally fed up with this badinage. My suggestion would be that we traverse the forest until we gain a reasonable exit route" said Marshwiz.

Then having agreed on their strategy, they forged on through the forest. In the far distance, they could still hear the minuscules, still arguing with each other.

Eventually, they emerged from the forest into blinding sunlight. Previously the forest had protected them from the harsh realities of the outside world. The intense temperature radiating from their sun deterred them from entering the parched plane that stretched in front of them.

"I am not certain on our next course of action. However, it seems that if we leave the shade of the forest, we may be scorched out of existence. Therefore, our only option is to remain within the confines of the forest and skirt round the periphery" said Marshwiz.

"I absolutely concur, the area outside the forest seems to be an arid death trap. There seems to be no wildlife and seems to consist mainly of desert and scrubland" replied Chiplet.

Having agreed on their next course of action, they both set out, yet remaining within the confines of the forest. Their progress became more limited, as their way was being continuously blocked by huge, uprooted trees. Some of the trees blocking their path were so massif that they were forced to clamber over them. Then in the distance they heard a voice that seemed to be bellowing out words of perpetual enjoyment. As they approached nearer, to the vocalist, the voice became deafening. Then they rounded a corner and observed an incredible sight. There was this gigantic man sitting in what appeared to be a vast pool. More amazingly still, was the continual shower of water that poured down on him from what appeared to be a permanent hole in the sky. His voice wasn't in the slightest melodic. All that he was doing was repeating the same two words over and over, again.

"Who is this guy? He seems to be having a repetition problem. He keeps repeating bum and tit incessantly without any rhythm. However, he is colossal and probably twenty times larger than we are, so I suggest that we leave him alone" said Chiplet.

This proved to be an impossibility as the giant caught sight of them and immediately stood up, water cascading from him. Yet, from the permanent hole in the sky, the water continued to gush down on top of him.

"Greetings" roared out the giant. "As you are probably aware I don't receive many visitors, it's probably due to my naked state and my grotesque manners. However, I do provide a service to provide the correct answer to any question you may ask me," said the giant.

"Well, that sounds of great interest to us. However, there are at least a couple of questions that I would like to put to you" said Marshwiz.

"Then fire ahead with your questions", said the indolent giant.

His massive body was sprawled across the entire length of the bathing pool as if he hadn't a care in the world.

"Fine, then my first question must be, who are you and how did you arrive here?. My second would be that there appears to be a hole in the sky from which a constant supply of water pours down. How is this happening?" demanded Marshwiz.

"OK, in answer to your first question I really haven't a clue how I arrived here. I don't remember where I was ensconced in my previous world, except I do recollect inhabiting a vast stone palace. Then all I remember is materialising in this large grotto a few weeks ago. In reply to your second question, that turned out to be quite peculiar. The large grotto was without any water and was completely dry. I peered up at the roof of the grotto and complained that it was dry and should have access to water. I then heard a voice in the distance say 'Granted'. Then with an almighty crash, a large section of the roof fell in. I had to adroitly jump out of the way, to avoid injury. Almost immediately a constant flow of water poured down from a hole in the sky. It does appear to have magical properties, as my pool is always full but never overflows," said the giant.

"Yes, I can probably accept your explanation of how you arrived on the planet. We also seem to have been projected here in an almost identical way. However, I do find that your explanation of some kind of a mystical plumber, who supplies you with a never-ending supply of water, is a bit farfetched" said Chiplet.

"Yes, I echo your comments entirely" agreed Marshwiz.

"Well, I have summoned this creature before, when he granted me a never-ending supply of water. Perhaps, he may even put in a physical appearance to put your minds at rest," said the giant.

The giant then put his massive hands together and pressed them as if in prayer.

"I am not certain who you are, or what you actually represent. A few weeks ago, you granted me the gift of perpetual water. Unfortunately, some new arrivals don't believe in your powers and requested that I endeavour to summon you to make a physical appearance. You may of course, not wish to do this, if so, I fully understand," said the giant.

"Nothing seems to be happening, perhaps this supposed god is on holiday somewhere," said Chiplet.

Then, where in the past, the sunlight had been trying to break through the trees, it became entirely overcast and threatening. Then the brooding heavens unleashed themselves. Torrential rain smashed down on them; this was followed by a rumble of thunder. It was then that the elements really let rip. Both sheet and forked lightning sizzled their way across the heavens and then as suddenly as it had begun it stopped abruptly. Tranquillity and calm replaced the frantic activity of the violent storm.

Then a powerful voice cleaved through the silence.

"You approached me with a request to show my physical presence. Unfortunately, I am unable to perform that feat and lies far beyond my existing powers. Perhaps I owe you both a reasonable explanation. I am in fact a disembodied entity and have no natural form. Like both of you, I metamorphosed into a nebulous being situated in the clouds above the planet. However, I was gifted with a powerful voice, which has enabled me to communicate with you. I was also gifted with the thunder and lightning special effects, in order to make a dramatic appearance in front of you. Yet again I have no rational explanation for this gift. It seems that there is a supreme god that is intent on controlling all our destinies," said the cloud.

"That is most peculiar, it now appears that the cloud is just part of a never-ending mystery, that must be linked to an omnipotent being, that controls all our needs," said Marshwiz.

"Well, there is just one more thing that I should impart to you. Somehow this supreme being has lodged something in my consciousness. It wants you to continue with your journey. You must venture across the burning hot desert until you reach the temple of your dreams," said the cloud.

"This is getting weirder the longer you stay here, my head seems to be aching with the complexity of the situation," said the giant.

Then, having bid farewell to the giant and thanked him for his help,

both intrepid explorers decided to confer on their current situation.

"It seems to me that our options are few and far between. If we are to be guided by the cloud's instructions, we should set out immediately and traverse the scorching desert" said Marshwiz.

"Yes, I fully understand your trepidations, but I really feel that it is possibly our best option" replied Chiplet.

Then, having retraced their steps and clambered over fallen trees that blocked their passage, they finally emerged into the blistering sun of the desert. In the meantime, Chiplet had been quite busy and had gone into the fabrication industry. He had managed to detach several fronds from the palms, that had inserted themselves into the forest, from the nearby desert. He arrived flourishing his newly manufactured sunshades and rested them against a tree. He had managed to secure his improvised sunshades with twine from plant fibres. Marshwiz congratulated Chiplet on his ingenuity. Then having hefted Chiplet onto her shoulder she strode forward into the blazing sunshine. As they emerged from the shade of the forest, the ravening heat hit them with intense fervour. Marshwiz had managed to make decent progress and was approaching a large outcrop of rock when something moved in front of her. It was a voracious sand lizard. Marshwiz jumped back hurriedly whilst the sand lizard viewed her curiously. This was a huge creature displaying segmented body armour and a spiked tail. Chiplet who was following her was almost knocked over by her rapid movement. The sand lizard, who was twice the size of Marshwiz, seemed to find the whole episode very amusing. He had cavernous jaws and razor-sharp teeth.

"Don't you worry your pretty little head, I have just had lunch and I am not going to eat you" said the sand lizard.

"Well, I had already determined that, as most sand lizards are perfect gentlemen" replied Marshwiz.

"Now, that is a most surprising comment as I am the last of my kind. Where did you hear such a tale?" said the sand lizard.

"If I remember correctly, it must have been a general observation," said Marshwiz.

"Then, it was probably made a long time ago, as, after I depart all of my kind will be extinct," said the sand lizard.

"This is a blisteringly hot and dry desert. Where exactly are you heading for in such an inhospitable region? "said the sand lizard.

Then Marshwiz explained about the cloud which had instructed them to venture across the desert until you reach the temple of your dreams.

The sand lizard advised them to be ultra-careful, as there were many nightmare creatures in the scorching sands. They both bade him farewell and continued with their journey.

Under the shade of the parasol, they deliberated if it would be better to travel at night and away from the glare of the sun. They then decided that it was probably far better to travel in broad daylight, as at least they could identify any nightmare beasties, that may be prowling around. Chiplet insisted on carrying the parasol which shaded both of them from the intense rays of the sun. In the distance they picked up the sound of a forcing out of air, closely followed by a huge belch. They mounted a vast sand dune and peered over the top. Lying in an enormous sand bowl was a grotesque flabby creature. The enormous belch that had spewed forth from its enormous mouth, was probably caused by the vast amount of sand toads, that it had been guzzling down. The nightmarish aspect of the situation was that the creature had involved itself in cannibalism and was devouring members of his family tree. The foul odour of the massive belch was still drifting up to them and lingered on the still air.

"What an evil dreadful creature devouring his own kind. I think that I really should do something about his morals and teach him a short sharp lesson" said Chiplet.

"But the foul thing is absolutely enormous. What do you intend to do?" questioned Marshwiz.

"Well, I have been thinking of the best way to approach the problem and believe that I have found a solution. Initially, I spent a great deal of time in fashioning the elaborate parasol. Then, to pierce the ground I sharpened the end of the parasol. It is my intention to descend to where the slobbering creature resides and to pierce its foul body with the implement" said Chiplet.

Full of admiration, Marshwiz observed Chiplet's rapid descent to confront the beast. He was flourishing the pointed parasol as if it were a deadly weapon. Hovering above the giant sand toad, was a yellow haze of putrid slime, that had emanated from the creature's body. Chiplet waded through the slime to reach his final goal. He then poised his improvised weapon above the giant sand toad and stabbed down several times. An ominous rumbling began to emanate from the sand toad's body. An alarmed Chiplet jumped back hurriedly and began sprinting back up the hill. The rumbling noise became more intense and there was an instant silence. This was followed by a massive explosion and stinking yellow, foul-smelling rain, deluged down on both of them.

"Well, I suppose that we should be grateful for small mercies, from the look of the yellow rain I thought that we may be in for a heavy shower of concentrated acid" said Marshwiz.

"Yes, and I could see that we would have had a huge problem with that, as I left the parasol stuck in the innards of the foul beastie. Maybe I should have extracted it, to give you some protection against the yellow rain" said Chiplet.

Marshwiz, quite liked the idea that he was feeling protective of her and it made her tingle all over.

They were already many days into their journey as they headed onward in their quest for the temple of dreams. The sun was roasting them in its glare, as they no longer had the protection of the parasol. As they came to the brow of yet another dune, they noticed something white and fluttering in the valley below. When they reached the white object, they realised that it consisted of some mystical material. However, it was of an exceedingly large size. Chiplet discovered a long length of wood nearby and managed to poke it through the material. He then draped it over both their heads and formed a canopy. Thus, protected from the intense temperature of the sun they made good progress. They were forced to slow down when they spotted a flock of birds on the horizon in front of them.

"Well, there seems to be quite a few of them and they are fairly large and they appear to be attacking something on the ground in front of them," said Marshwiz.

"Then, whatever is down there, probably needs our assistance" retorted Chiplet.

They were able to see clearly that the creature under attack had managed to fend off the attacking birds. Both of them charged down the hill shouting and screaming as they approached. The flock of birds, having been alerted to their arrival, took one look at the enormous white flapping object that was approaching them and scattered in all directions. Having arrived in front of the creature, they began to study it intently. This creature was far smaller than its rescuers and was incredibly hairy. A welcoming smile had spread across its features and when it smiled the whole planet smiled with it.

"Greetings and thank you both for your timely rescue. I was getting pecked unmercifully by those beastly birds. By the way, my name is Sunny" said a smiling Sunny.

"Yes, it is pretty simple to guess your birth name, you appear to be a very happy individual. You also seem to have a permanent smile transfixed across your face. By the way what kind of creature are you?" Questioned Chiplet.

"My species are called the Sunny," said Sunny.

"But that is your name" interjected Marshwiz.

"You are absolutely correct. It is most definitely my name, but having said that I am a very rare type of species. So rare in fact that as far I am aware, I am the only one that exists," said Sunny.

"That is interesting and makes you totally unique. However, we are endeavouring to find a mystical place known as The Temple of your dreams. Have you any idea where this place maybe?" Questioned Marshwiz.

"Well, believe it or not, I do confer quite often with a well-travelled avian called the traveller bird. He informed me that on several occasions he had flown over an enormous temple adorned by numerous minarets and probably part of a mosque. Could this be The Temple of your dreams? If it is, you must carry on towards the setting sun and never deviate from your journey," said Sunny.

They left the happy smiling hairy creature and continued with their journey.

"How is it that a being like Sunny is able to spread such happiness around him? Even when he was around, although it was for such a short time, I had a permanent smile transfixed across my visage" said Chiplet.

"Yes, it was very strange. I too had this weird compulsion to envisage that all things were beautiful, and everything would turn out to be wonderful "said Chiplet.

Both flew onwards towards the setting sun, following their instructions and not deviating from their course in anyway. A peculiarity of their planet was that because of their planet's position on its solar orbit, it appeared that the sun was very often setting. However, it still gave them a focal point to aim for. They flew on and sometimes glided and covered huge distances on their seemingly interminable quest.

Many of the birds and animals they encountered, were of an entirely different species. The most flamboyant of the avians was the firebird. This was a creature with a very short life expectancy. Unfortunately, they had a habit of exploding in massive explosions of fire. None of the avians dared venture too close to it, because of this dangerous habit. But there again the planet had a way of preserving its inhabitants. In its atmosphere, it reassembled the molecules from the charred remains of the firebird. Then breathed new life into it and a new firebird was instantly created. Peculiarly enough, in the far distance, they viewed one of these amazing birds but decided to veer away from it. Then, they spotted strange warthog-looking animals but realized that they were not a sentient species and would be unable to communicate with them. They both decided to land by a crystal clear lake. However, when they landed, the lake had disappeared, and they had landed in a dust bowl. They had obviously been misled by a mirage, having been utterly fooled by the planet's whim.

"Well, we seem to be putting in a great deal of endeavours without getting any satisfactory results. However, at least we can carry on in the supposed correct direction towards the setting sun" complained Marshwiz.

"Do you know, I have thoroughly enjoyed our adventure and you are an exceedingly good companion to have along" said Chiplet.

Then having escaped from the mirage, the intrepid explorers foraged onwards. Marshwiz was also feeling that she had been incredibly lucky in her choice of companion. Their journey continued and yet for the first time they encountered mountains. Both had to fly over high peaks, which guarded a vast range of mountains. There was an expanse of ground that was completely covered in freezing white stuff. Then more of the white stuff started falling directly out of the sky. It had been incredibly cold in the mountains, and they were glad to eventually emerge on the red-hot plains of the desert. However, on the horizon ahead of them spread out an even more welcoming view. It was the vista of a magnificent city, which was dominated by a wonderfully domed temple. The exquisite dome flashed out a million different colours in the dying rays of the setting sun.

"Well, it looks like we may have arrived at our destination. The Te m p l e of dreams" said Marshwiz.

"Yes, you could be correct in your assumption. What a fantastic city this is, in its originality and splendour. It is absolutely mind-blowing" said Chiplet.

Both stared transfixed at the cityscape, that sprawled out in front of them. It seemed to sprawl onwards forever. The city lights were flickering before them.

"At last, you have arrived, we have been waiting for your arrival for eternity" declared a massive voice from the heavens.

"OK, and now that we have arrived what exactly do you desire from us?" enquired anxious Chiplet.

"We require absolutely nothing, after all, it is your own destiny that you must fulfil. Both of you will be left to your own devices, without any interference. You are not an experiment but a source of new sentient life for this planet" said the voice.

Both Marshwiz and Chiplet settled down on the outskirts of the Temple of dreams and had many children. They enjoyed great happiness together and lived long and fruitful life.

Ad infinitum.

LUCKY JOE

In a galaxy a trillion light years from planet earth, existed a planet that was a mirror image of planet earth. As so often occurred as the result of a mirror image planet, lived a doppelganger individual called Lucky Joe, which was hardly surprising as he was incredibly lucky. If he was to toss a coin in the air and call heads, he would always be 100 per cent correct. He would sometimes have a flutter on the horses and always was the victor. However, he restrained himself from wagering too heavily as he would put the bookies out of business and that wouldn't have been in his own interest. Another of his favourite pastimes was roulette. There again, they would spin the wheel and his number would always come up. He had realised that his incredibly good fortune was not the norm. Poker was a card game that Joe was really excited about. However, it became really strange when a voice in his head informed him exactly the cards that his opponent was holding in his hand. The whole situation was to become quite weird, and he deliberately lost numerous hands of poker, so as not to upset his opponent.

It was at this time that he decided to enter the national lottery and try his luck. Immediately that he sat down at his desk a flood of numbers poured into his brain. He then digested the numbers and selected his choice. Unfortunately, his selection of numbers was the same selection of numbers as millions of other punters. However, he wasn't in the slightest dismayed and the following week he utilized the same procedure. Yet again the numbers flashed into his inner being and he selected his choice. However, this time he was the only winner. Then over the next few months, he repeated the process time after time. Joe began to garner literally millions of dollars. Now he decided was the time for clever investment. As he had become exceedingly wealthy, he had billions to invest. Yet again it was his brain that controlled his every choice. It instructed him on how to make his investment wisely and without risk. It was then that Joe began to realise that the real buzz that he used to get was because of the uncertainty of his gamble. Yet because of the numbers that constantly flooded his brain, it was impossible for him to lose. Yes, he was absurdly wealthy but also had become totally bored with life.

Joe then decided, as he motored on in his flash limousine, that his only option was to endeavour to lose. In order to do this, he completely ignored the numbers that kept flashing into his brain. Unfortunately, he soon discovered that it was to no avail, as he kept on winning. Distraught and uncertain about what his next move would be, he decided to abstain from any games of chance. However, there seemed to be this incessant voice in the back of his mind that urged him to participate in the game of chance and where is the harm in that? It was around this time that Joe became really depressed and sought sanctuary in a bottle. He became totally inebriated and passed out on several occasions. Eventually, he found error in his ways as the voice told him that he had been granted an incredible gift that he should use wisely. Joe heeded this advice and from that day onwards became a changed person.

After Joe's epiphany, he tried to avoid all types of gambling. Because of his amazing luck in the lottery, he was as rich as Croesus and invested his wealth wisely. He invested in the building industry and not only watched the buildings grow but his assets as well. However, deep in Joe's makeup was the innate need for excitement which had been sadly missing from his recent exploits. Then he decided that the only option open to him was to lose the billions that he had accumulated whilst playing the lottery. His endeavours to lose this money proved to be almost entirely fruitless. He started betting on horses that were rank outsiders and had high odds. Unfortunately, or fortunately, whichever way you want to view this, Joe won even more money. He had an enormous problem he was unable to lose. It was then that Joe decided that he needed help and visited a psychiatrist. However, when Joe explained his predicament to the psychiatrist, he was completely dumbfounded.

"You mean to tell me that you have a gambling problem, and you just can't lose. That doesn't seem like a problem to me, besides which I don't believe you," said the psychiatrist.

"Oh, you of little faith, then I will have to demonstrate it to you," said lucky Joe.

Joe then produced a coin from his pocket and flourished it as he did so.

"Well, you can probably observe that there is nothing untoward about this coin. It is not even my lucky coin but a random coin with no particular value. However, on one side of the coin, there is an effigy of a head and on the reverse side that of a tail. If I toss the coin and make a call. I will always be one hundred per cent correct" explained Lucky Joe.

The psychiatrist then asked, "What would happen if I were to make the call?" "Then, if you were to do so it would not make the slightest difference I would still win," said lucky Joe.

Then to add force to his claim, he tossed the coin, and the psychiatrist made more tosses and at each call lost the bet. To prove his point even more, they made a dozen coin tosses and each time the psychiatrist was the loser.

"Where are you going?" Demanded Joe.

"Well, after the experience that I have just witnessed and what you put me through, I am going to visit a good friend of mine who also happens to be a psychiatrist".

Lucky Joe was in a quandary and didn't know in which direction to turn. His problem was that he had to make a choice between good and evil. The reason was that Satan, the evil one, had appeared in a dream and offered him riches beyond his wildest dreams. Joe howled with laughter at the attempt to bribe him by the satanic overlord. Then informed him that he obviously hadn't been paying attention as he was already incredibly wealthy. Satan then asked him what would interest him if he would care to name a wish. Joe advised him that he was far above any type of temptation and that Satan should desist in his naive attempt to bribe him. With that, his satanic majesty disappeared in a blinding flash and a cloud of black smoke. Gosh, it seems that I have really upset the evil one and he is behaving like a pantomime villain, thought Joe. Then what could Joe do to rid himself of the malaise that seemed to be engulfing him? Perhaps the answer would be in a quest for speed on the motorbike that he had just purchased. Dangerous to the extremes with no thought for other road users, he hurtled around corners often on the wrong side of the road. Having just avoided nearly being involved in a massive pile-up, he then realizes that he was being silly and was not paying attention to the needs of other road users. Therefore, he decided to mend his ways. The pace that he had set himself was truly frantic and relentless and without any meaning. Whereas in the past he had thoroughly enjoyed his wagers he had lost the desire to indulge in any of his past misdemeanours. His problem was that as it seemed that it was impossible to lose, why bother with any type of wager? Joe had spent a particularly restless night when the evil one invaded his thought processes.

"You have become a major problem for me, but I believe that I may have solved our problem. This should be fairly easy to solve. The nightmare scenario that I encountered is that when you make a wager it is virtually impossible to lose. I believe that through various tweaking and manipulation that I will be able to do, I will be able to eliminate your lucky streak and convert you into an unfortunate loser," said the satanic voice.

"Are you absolutely certain that you would be able to do this as it will, remove a huge weight from my mind?" queried lucky Joe.

"Yes, I can categorically guarantee success in my elaborated scheme which will take away your winning streak permanently" boasted the satanic overlord.

"Well, it sounds to be the right path to follow. What do I have to do?" replied lucky Joe.

"You must do absolutely nothing and remain here," said the satanic overlord.

"You have been gifted with incredible luck and because of your ingratitude, I shall remove this gift forever" sneered the evil one.

Joe felt extremely lightheaded as the gift was removed from him. However, as he ventured across the road, he was squashed by a massive lorry.

The moral of this story is that you should look both ways when you cross the road or wait for the traffic lights to change.

Ad infinitum.

VAMPIRE

It seemed to be incredibly strange, but he was hanging upside down from a large wooden structure, as he would discover later, the structure was called a tree. There were literally a hundred or so of his brethren, hanging down from their varied perches. He was totally mystified about his behaviour and why he had adopted such an ungainly resting place. To add to his confusion there were plenty of other things called leaves, that semi-masked the siblings, hanging with him. He couldn't recollect how he had arrived there. He just knew that suddenly he existed.

He found out as he was just hanging about with nothing to do, that he had somehow been able to analyse everything around him. This gift had enabled him to discover many important issues, in fact, he had been granted intelligence. His knowledge expanded exponentially, thrusting new ideas and clarity upon him. He even understood the kind of creature that he was. He was a vampire bat. Information seemed to flood into his head from all angles.

On a planet known as Earth, which was a billion light years away from his current residence, an unholy creature had existed that sucked blood from its victims. During that time a plague existed, which was known as the black death. Victims of this dreadful scourge would haemorrhage and vomit blood in copious amounts. It was also known as bubonic plague which was transmitted by flees of the black rat and killed millions.

There was, however, another theory that a vampiric killer was the source of this outrage. As victims increased, the legend of a vampiric killer multiplied. This satanic creature became the embodiment of evil. His persona was that of a black-cloaked being with sharp pointed teeth. Red eyes glared out at the victim before he gauged himself on their blood. A ghastly fate awaited the victims, as they became the living dead. Having digested all this information,

Vamp woke up with a start and analysed his position. He had already decided to call himself Vamp, as he was in essence a vampire bat. He had no desire, to follow the wicked route, to dine exclusively on blood. The major reason was that he hadn't a clue, what blood actually was.

Vamp released himself from the tree, spread his wings and glided down to the ground. Having landed safely he strutted off on his muscular legs to investigate his surroundings. Suddenly the air around him became full of fluttering wings, as his colleague vampire bats, followed his route to the ground. Unfortunately, there was a mid-air collision between two of the bats, which lead to a violent confrontation. Vamp was dismayed by this aggressive behaviour but decided not to become involved. Then suddenly, he had this incredible yearning for the forbidden liquid blood. Then, he realised that the constant flow of information that had nestled in his mind must have influenced his thought processes. This led to his vampiric lust for blood. He strode onwards pondering the meaning of the new life that had been granted him.

However, his quest for the inexplicable came to a shuddering halt, as one of the tree-bearing vampires, landed in front of him and he had to dodge out of the way.

"Sorry about that, I wasn't watching what I was doing and almost thumped into you. Luckily, you managed to jump out of the way. By the way, I have called myself Spring, as I adore the thought of everything bursting into life again" said Spring.

"Well, you certainly didn't inflict any damage on me, and you seem as light as a feather," said Vamp.

"Where are you heading next? You seem to be an agreeable type to accompany on your journey," said Spring.

"I am not certain if it would be very wise of me to invite you along, as I seemed to have developed this insatiable lust for blood. My name is Vamp".

Spring fell in, alongside the massive striding Vamp and managed to match him stride for stride, as she floated along as gracefully as a feather. After continuing their journey for a few more hours, she thought it quite pertinent as Vamp hadn't replied to her original question, of demanding where they were heading for.

"We shall head in the direction, in which I can sense the strongest aroma of blood. The journey is lightly to be hazardous and fraught with danger. Are you sure, you still wish to accompany me on this perilous mission?" Questioned Vamp.

"Yes, thank you for your advice, but I have only just been created. I look forward to indulging myself in an exciting adventure," said Spring.

Having received his companion's admission, that she still wished to accompany him, they both headed out from under the trees and into a fertile valley. After a short period of time, they both decided to take to the air. There was only a light breeze so that made flying a doddle. The grasslands stretched on into the far distance and disappeared eventually, into the hazy horizon. However, they both descended quite rapidly, as a large avian materialized in the sky in front of them. Luckily, they had picked a rocky area with huge boulders adorning the summit.

"That avian is absolutely enormous. What do you think that it can be?" questioned Spring.

"Well, we seem to have arrived in the middle of a creation blitz. The prime example of this is both of us. This planet seems to be at the dawn of creation and the aerial being in front of us has probably just been created as well. I suggest that we wait and discover what exactly it is" suggested Vamp.

Unfortunately, the huge monster seemed to have entered into the zone of slomo and everything was grinding to a halt. Then they heard a massive crash and the ground pulsated around them. Vamp leapt up on one of the huge boulders and peered over the top in the direction of the noise. He then conveyed his findings to Spring.

"This creature is totally ridiculous and no wonder it was forced to make a crash landing. It's massive but has tiny little wings which obviously are unable to support its huge bulk. It's ungainly and although it is so vast, it also has the appearance of being unbalanced. When it smashed into the ground, it obviously inflicted some permanent damage on itself. There is a gigantic wound in its head, that is raining out a green substance. Added to this, it has a colossal beak that is lying at an odd angle. The salient truth of the matter is that it may have broken its neck," said Vamp.

In the meantime, Spring had clambered up on the boulder and was viewing the avian for herself. Vamp had described the condition of the wounded avian to perfection. She could immediately analyse from the twitching and contortions of the avian that it was in an extremely bad way.

"What do you intend to do?" Said Spring.

"There is nothing that we can do. This avian is dying, whether we like it or not. It seems to me, that whoever created this misfortunate creature, seems to have mixed up all the pieces. The result is the emergence of a creature with no hope. I suggest that we carry on with our journey and leave this creature behind," said Vamp.

Then only too glad to escape from the locality of the dying avian, they both flew off. Their intention was to continue the search for the mystical substance known as blood. On the horizon a jagged mountain range sprang up in front of them, they forged on towards the mountains. As neither of them required sustenance, their energy levels were always fully charged. They continued on in the direction of the mountains, until night-time fell, shutting out the burning sun. Although they both possessed amazing night vision, they decided to hunker down for the night. They had spotted a large tree and they hung down from its branches in perfect unison.

A few hours later their sun was starting to roast them and forced them to evacuate their previously comfortable perch. The mountains were beginning to loom nearer when ahead of them appeared a noisy flock of avians. Vamp who was twice their size flew directly at them and scattered them in all directions. This was a terrible mistake, as a voice boomed down at him.

"You miserable worm, why are you attacking my babies?" said an angry voice.

Vamp hearing the voice moved rapidly to one side as the angry mother swept past him. She was twice his size and was seeking retribution. Luckily for Vamp she was so large that she lacked his manoeuvrability.

Spring, having witnessed Vamp's silly antics from afar, was roaring with laughter and followed him to a safe distance away from the vengeful mother.

"Well, that was an exceedingly difficult situation, that you bailed yourself out from. I didn't realise you were such a bully until I witnessed your attack on her babies," said Spring.

"That is totally unfair, those so-called babies of hers were extremely annoying and very large" replied Vamp.

"Mind you the way that you fled, to escape the vengeful mother, was truly heroic" giggled Spring.

Vamp decided that he had taken enough mockery from Spring and took to the air. He was followed shortly after by a still chortling Spring. Vamp was still tracking the heady fragrance of blood that assailed his senses. Occasionally they descended to the ground to assess the situation. They noted that the mighty mountains were marching towards them, at great speed. The foothills of the mountain range soon encroached on their vision. However, they were totally unprepared for the gigantic creature that lumbered into view. It had the same status as a small mountain but was incredibly slow-moving. They had decided to land, to investigate this extraordinary behemoth.

"Look at the size of it, it's no wonder that it is such a ponderous mover. It has a massive pair of horns that are firmly embedded in a massive skull. It has an extremely shaggy coat that appears to comprise of matted hair. What sex it is, is almost impossible to distinguish. It doesn't really matter, as it's so slow moving it would take a year to reach us," said Vamp.

It was just then, that the creature seemed to fix him with a baleful stare and bellowed. Almost immediately, in the far distance came a reciprocating bellow.

"Well, that really does capture the imagination, there must be at least two of them. How do they copulate, without trampling each other to death?" said Spring.

"Yes, you have just proved to me, that you really do have a vivid imagination. With all that trampling going on, it must be terribly exciting for you" said a smirking Vamp.

"That is so unfair, that comment was made because of your cowardly attack on the mothers' babies" retorted Spring.

"You are absolutely correct in your assumption. I could have been killed or severely maimed by that vengeful mother and all you did was howl with laughter" exploded Vamp.

"Then, I must apologise for my heartless behaviour I think you are terrific, and I totally admire you," said Spring.

"Yeah, I suppose that it did have its funny side and as long as you totally admire me, there is no harm done" replied a smiling Vamp.

The land had transformed itself and the burning arid land had been replaced by green pastures. They continued with their epic journey, mostly in flight over the green and pleasant land. Occasionally, they would descend to the pastures to discuss their current predicament, which was really an excuse to escape from hours of tedious flying. In the sky ahead of them, appeared a flock of brightly coloured crimson birds. Having been surprised on a couple of occasions previously, they approached with caution. It was just as well they did. The crimson bird nearest to them exploded with a huge blast. Totally aghast at the occurrence, they descended to the ground to discuss the situation.

"Our planet seems to be getting weirder and weirder. For our private entertainment, they seem to have provided exploding firebirds. They seem to be fairly large. I wonder if they reach adulthood before they explode," said Vamp.

"Yes, I see exactly what you mean. These are gorgeous birds with a limited life span, that are living on the edge in perpetuity," said Spring.

She had barely finished her sentence when another crimson bird exploded. Thereafter pandemonium reigned, as bird after bird exploded. It seemed that with the continuance of the explosions, it had become synchronised. However, they had noticed that although all the birds had exploded, there was no sign of the beautiful birds, not even a feather.

"Well, it has become obvious what the planet is doing. Everything that it has created, it destroys if there is a problem with its makeup. Then it probably reassembles the molecules and creates another creature. It is obviously working under the premise that if it doesn't work, let's recycle it" replied Vamp.

"Yeah, I can agree with you on that assumption. The only good thing about it is that it has left us to our own devices. Perhaps it thinks that we are perfect," said Spring.

"Well, perfect is in the eye of the beholder. Therefore, in your case I can vouch for your fascinating beauty" said Vamp.

"When do you think that we will get there wherever that may be?" demanded Spring.

"Yeah, that is a very pertinent question and my response is I haven't the faintest idea. The scent of blood seemed to linger in the air and urges me onwards, and then it vanishes. I will fully understand if you wish to give up the quest and go your separate way" replied Vamp.

"For me, that is not an option, you were perfectly correct when you suggested that the journey would be perilous. But then what excitement and adventures we have had together. You can't get rid of me that easily. I will continue our journey," said Spring.

They both had decided that flying to their destination, was by far the easiest method. Yet another range of mountains had materialised in the far distance as they continued with their aerial mission. The landscape had dramatically changed again. The verdant grasses had disappeared, to be replaced by a burning desert. Then, in the distance they heard a roaring noise, that got louder as they approached closer. A cleft opened in the rockface in front of them, leading into a valley that hosted a monumental waterfall. The sound was deafening, as they flew around the rockface of the cascade. Magical rainbows appeared in the spray, induced by the planet's sun. They exited the valley and emerged into a vast lake, that was fed by the thundering torrent, they had left behind them.

They had barely emerged from the valley, when a huge fish with gaping jaws, tried to snatch them out of the sky. They located a small island and landed on it.

"Well, that was exciting, that fish was massive. He only just missed, you would have made a lovely meal" said Vamp.

"Yes, that was a close shave. However, I know that you would have dived in and rescued me" replied Spring.

"That is where you are so wrong. This lake is crammed full of voracious fish, waiting for their next meal. No, you would be on your own" said Vamp.

However, having stated his intention, she look so crestfallen, that he rapidly retracted it. They flew off the island and continued over the lake, which was immense and seemed to reach on forever. They passed over a monster fish, that was in the process of devouring some of his kind, of a smaller variety of itself. The expanse of the lake seemed to be interminable, and they were flying over water for ages. Eventually, they arrived at the end of the lake and flew over a dense forest. They then passed over a selection of orchards. It became perfectly obvious to the two highflyers and had also become ingrained in their minds, that they were passing over a fruit-growing area. They descended to analyse their findings and landed on a grassy bank.

"Well, we seem to be flying over vast expanses of varied fruits. But I must admit for the first time, I got an incredibly strong whiff of blood. We seem to be heading in the right direction" said Vamp.

"Then you must be extremely happy, that you have almost reached your journey's end" replied Spring.

"No, not really happy. I have enjoyed your company throughout our hazardous adventures, although your constant exuberance was quite waring, for some of the time. Besides this, I would like to point out, that although I can scent the heady fragrance of blood, where is it emanating from?" Said Vamp.

Then having partaken of the slight sojourn, they rose into the sky yet again. The fields of fruit were changing colour from pale yellow to a dramatic red. Suddenly without warning Vamp swooped down out of the sky and landed between the trees that were festooned with startling red fruit. He then started jumping up and down with excitement. In the meantime, Spring had landed beside him.

"I have found it" he shouted out with joy "I have found blood" screamed Vamp.

In the next instance a gale-force wind blew up and lightning zapped across the sky above them

"Sorry about the special effects, but they really caught your attention" boomed a thunderous voice.

"Both of you survived and passed your test admirably. You are both two of the cleverest beings, that I have been able to manufacture. Regarding you Vamp, I am afraid that I totally misled you. I fed into your newly created mind, the legend of the evil Vampire. This creature had an incessant lust for blood, which I also instilled in you. Hence, the constant craving and lust for blood. However, I did alter your profile somewhat, not wishing to create a malicious blood-sucking monster. You have attained your desire Vamp for blood and are standing in an orchard of blood oranges. It seems, therefore, that I have created a being with a lust for exotic fruit.

"Yes, I have made ghastly mistakes with my creations. My intention is to head for another planet in our galaxy and create perfection. From this moment on, you will be on your own, without any interference from me" said the thunderous voice.

"Well, that was simply astonishing and almost beyond belief. He used the word manufactured as if he was able to stick us together in component parts. Could this be true?" Queried Spring.

"Well, it seems to me that this guy is omnipotent. He obviously created me and decided to give me a lust for blood. This turned out to be blood oranges. I think that he was boasting about it. I am sure that he was chortling in the background. However, the good news is, that he has in all probability disappeared forever. That leaves me asking the pertinent question, what are we going to do with the rest of our lives?" Said Vamp.

"Yes, I am glad that you asked me that. I have been your constant companion over vast stretches of time and have learned to trust and love you. With this in mind I would like to give birth to tiny batlings" said Spring.

Many light years from planet earth, exists a world that is populated by wondrous creatures. The predominant species are vampire bats. If you are lucky enough to encounter this planet, you will be greeted with warmth and affection.

Ad infinitum.

MR PUTRID

Mr. Putrid lived with his wife and two children in stinky poo ally. Mr. Putrid was born in a world that stank of a multitudinous variety of smells. Never having been introduced to the luxury of sanitation, he was quite happy to exist in a world of incredibly toxic odours. His crescent backed onto a large block of toilets that was frequently used by a group of rat buggers, large and impolite creatures.

Mr. Putrid emerged from his privately designed hell hole and breathed in the wonderful stinking odours of the Stink-Opolis, the amazing city that he lived in. His wife was called Flusher, as she had the dreadful inclination of flushing the multitude of toilets that were in her vicinity. Putrid's two kids were named Sniff and Spit, which they seemed to be doing constantly. Mr. Putrid's neighbour was exceedingly well educated and owned a chemist shop, well stocked with disgustingly smelling toiletries. His biggest selling product was 'Poo de Excrement' which was foul smelling. Mr. Putrid was of small size. However, he possessed a huge head and pointed nose which seemed to be intent on investigating anything that entered his vision. His mouth was enormous and displayed row after row of broken yellow teeth.

As Mr. Putrid and Sniff and Spit ventured on down their friendly neighbourhood street, they were forced to kick the garbage and the occasional dead cat out of heir way. Finally, they arrived at the large market square that sold everything that Mr. Putrid utilised in his everyday existence. One of the stallholders a large florid man acknowledged Putrid with a cursory wave of his hand. Immediately Mr. Putrid went over to his store and purchased two hundred fart explosions. He had an ulterior motive for his purchase, as he was always being accused of letting one off in public. His thought was as he was constantly accused of this foul act, he would create mayhem by letting off fifty fart explosions at the same time. Yes, he would probably be accused of farting in public. Then on the other hand it couldn't possibly be him, with such a multitude of farting invading the neighbourhoods. His two boys were giggling inanely in the background as he set off the fart explosions. They then rushed back down the street roaring with laughter at the sheer audacity of their actions. As they shot round the corner, they were confronted by the local bobby PC Nosy Parker.

"Hello, hello," he said, Policemen tend to say that. "What have we here?"

"Sorry officer we shouldn't have been rushing so much, but we were trying to escape from the machinations of the fart maestro," said Putrid.

"Well, I don't believe that I have ever heard of him. Is he dangerous?" demanded Parker.

"That very much depends on how you approach him. He doesn't like being surprised by anyone and takes drastic action if needs to" said Putrid.

"Sounds particularly dangerous to me, perhaps I should arrest him. What action does he perform, to make himself so dangerous to the public" demanded Parker?

"That is extremely easy to answer. He has this propensity to deliver exploding fart balls in their thousands, to an unsuspecting audience" replied Putrid.

"What a terrible individual, if I catch up with him, I shall certainly clap him into jail," said Parker.

After the unsuspecting officer had departed, Putrid and his two sons broke into howls of laughter.

"What a dingbat, the guy is so stupid that he would be scared of his own shadow," said Putrid.

All three of them trundled their way home. Then it started to snow, and their footprints remained firmly imprinted on the surface. Putrid misjudged his stride and slipped on the ice which hurtled him into an iron barrier and he hit it with a sickening crunch. He screamed in agony as his two sons rushed to his side. Unfortunately, they were too late, and Mr. Putrid died on the spot.

The moral of this story is, if you are serious about anything, don't fart around too long or your dream may explode in your face.

Ad infinitum.

TREES

Beneath the canopy of the massive oak trees, nothing stirred. The forest was totally enmeshed in stygian darkness. The silence was deafening, encouraged by its threatening lack of movement. These trees were different trees from other parts of the forest, they had been gifted with arboreal intelligence and were nightwalkers. Garth, who considered himself to be the leader of the tree people, took a ponderous step forward and in unity, his companions followed his giant steps. This was a dangerous forest to inhabit. A massive slither bug with fearsome appendages appeared from nowhere and crashed into Garth. However, he felt nothing but a slight irritation that this insignificant creature had been so clumsy. The nightwalkers were now emerging from the forest and underneath a night sky that was ablaze with the suns from a billion different worlds. The nightwalkers assembled on an escarpment overlooking a valley, there were over four hundred of them. The nightwalkers had received a special gift from the maker of all things. They were all telepathic and were able to commune with each other. A thousand comets danced across the night sky seemingly heralding the arrival of these thousand-foot trees. The tree folk themselves buzzed with excitement as all their thoughts collided with each other. Eventually, Garth's patience ran out. He boomed out his thoughts,

'Desist and be silent.' The hubbub ceased almost immediately. 'Treekin brethren, as you all know, we only dare venture out at night when the skies darken. This is because of the dreadful threat we would encounter should we emerge in the daylight hours.

'These gigantic creatures, we call the log biters, would rip and shred your bodies to a pulp. Therefore, we remain within the sanctuary of the forest.'

There was complete silence as Garth's comments were digested by the nightwalkers. Then a thought invaded Garth's mind.

'Should we not defend ourselves against these creatures whom we know nothing about? Although they do say the best form of defence is attack.'

Garth then realised that the invading suggestion had arrived from a little oak tree called Whisp. He had no intention of offending her and replied accordingly.

'I understand your bitterness Whisp and as we look down this valley there isn't a log biter in sight. However, when our sun is in its ascendancy, they emerge and start ripping and shredding. Only last week at the north end of the forest a group of nightwalkers similar to us made the grave mistake of loitering out too long. We picked up their screams of anguish as they were smashed into small bits. No Whisp, I think that the sanctuary of the forest is still our best bet. We had better return to our sanctuary before we get attacked by these monsters'.

Having returned to the forest Garth realised just how dangerous for his clan it had been. An example of this was one of the most dangerous denizens of the forest was the snort slicer. This was a huge animal over eighty feet in height which trapped its prey by snorting out a viscous fluid from its elongated trunk and glueing them to the forest floor. It would then leisurely slice its victims into small pieces and devour them. Luckily, this creature is quite rare and there are only a few of them. Yet another giant predator, was the worm crusher. These would call the log biters, who would rip and shred bodies to a pulp. Therefore, Garth had decided to remain within the sanctuary of the forest in safety from these creatures whom he knew nothing about.

One of the many monsters, he knew they were up against was the smudge crusher. It encircled its prey and crushed it to resemble a flattened smudge. However, it made little impression on the nightwalkers because of their gigantic frames. There were other predators of a much smaller stature which held little fear to the nightwalkers.

Garth, however, kept returning to Whisp's comment that the best form of defence was attack. She was young, he thought to himself and headstrong and had much to learn. At the moment a frontal attack on the log biters would not be a good idea. He also knew from other encounters with the tree folk, that the forest was vast and extended way beyond his imagination. Garth then decided that the best option for the group of nightwalkers would be to explore the other side of the forest and venture as far as they were able to go. He assembled the group of nightwalkers together and explained to them his reasoning.

A few hours later the towering tree folk were smashing through the forest endeavouring to reach the other side. A small gaggle of cone sniffers scurried away in front of them whilst trying to escape. As far as the nightwalkers were concerned, they barely noticed them. Garth and his companions were totally self-sustaining and required no nourishment. They internally manufactured a super protein that powered their huge frames. Garth was leading the contingent of his tree brethren when they crashed into an enormous clearing and came to a shuddering halt. There in front of them was a gigantic creature. However, in comparison to Garth the eighty-foot-high snort slicer, was still a diminutive entity. Garth was not a believer in reputations however lurid they may be. and stamped down hard on the snort slicer. When a thousand-foot oak tree stamps hard, the recipient stays stamped. Observing the situation under his massive root, a horrible sticky mess had appeared. Had Garth been endowed with nasal appendages, he would have smelt the most diabolical odour. The nightwalkers continued their journey and although they were oblivious to time, they were able to sense the difference between night and day. Garth realised that the rotation between night and day had already occurred on multiple occasions. The nightwalkers carried on with their journey and their exciting adventure. Eventually, Griswold who was the oldest of the nightwalkers deemed it necessary to make a comment.

'Where are we going?' was his simple question.

'I don't know but I will tell you when we get there' was Garth's immediate response.

The trees plodded grimly onwards, many of them thinking that they were partaking in a lost cause. Just ahead of them Garth could sense a break in the skyline of the forest and then they hit daytime and emerged on a strip of sand. In front of them, they could sense a truly magical world of glimmering shapes and colours. They also sensed a vast expanse of water that stretched to the far horizon. A large corpulent creature lay indolently in the water. Huge tusks and whiskers adorned these blubber-enhanced monsters. Garth instantly named them, the whiskered blubber monsters. Occasionally waves broke over these magical creatures and different coloured rainbows played across each of their magical hides. Then as instantly as they had appeared, the rainbows disappeared again. Then they reappeared again as the magical light show continued in perpetuity and probably since the beginning of time. Garth and his companions were transfixed by the spectacle and being trees were literally rooted to the ground. Then on the far horizon, an even more prodigious figure emerged and everything in the minds of the nightwalkers instantly went into lockdown and for a moment in time, their world became frozen.

A voice exploded in the minds of the nightwalkers.

'All of you must follow the shoreline for ten thousand paces, where you will discover a large wooden floating barge that you must board. This will convey all of you to your next destination.'

Garth and his companions set out on their long journey around the headland. They had already left the whiskered blubber monsters far behind. Garth could hear the numerous telepathic conversations that were whirling around in his head and chose to ignore most of them. However, there was a more insistent voice that invaded his brain synapses. It was Whisp again who seemed to be frightened of the extent of their journey.

Griswold told her not to be so silly, as under the excellent leadership of Garth they would get there anyway.

'Then where are we actually going?' Griswold was forced to admit that he had not a clue, but he would tell her when they arrived there.

As they advanced down the strand, a line of medium-sized creatures shot out of the forest and blocked the way in front of them. Garth estimated that there were at least four thousand of them. Then they started pelting the oncoming tree folk with brown heavy objects which exploded, leaving a milky fluid when they smashed into the mighty nightwalkers. The nightwalkers did not even break their stride and the hurlers of the strange objects hastily disappeared back into the forest. It was still daylight when the nightwalkers reached their objective.

When they finally reached it, Garth was totally astounded by the vast size of the barge. He had surmised that his contingent must be travelling across water somewhere and it was obviously able to contain almost double their numbers. As previously instructed, they climbed into the huge high-sided vessel and steadied themselves.

The voice again permeated their minds.

'Brace yourselves we are leaving for the promised land.'

The next instant the massive craft was heading through the water at breakneck speed. Garth realised that something strange and wonderful was taking place. However, the idea of propulsion was way beyond his most vivid imagination. They forged on with their journey for many days and nights. The comprehension of time for these travellers was meaningless. These tree folks had no need for sustenance as the super protein in their massive frames allowed them as much energy as they needed.

On the fourth day, a fearsome long-necked creature with razor-sharp teeth soared into the air above. It was at least two thousand feet long. It yawned and spat out a great tendril of fire which hit the barge and started smouldering. Then there was a clap of thunder and a huge hand reached down from the sky above and hurled the dragon away from their craft. Garth heard a mighty chuckle and a voice from inside his head said,

'You naughty beasty'.

There was immediate pandemonium within the ranks of the nightwalkers. However, there was one ruling they all agreed on. This omnipotent supernatural being in the sky above must be the maker of all things. They voyaged onwards passing through the eye of a storm and many hurricanes. An enormous white floating thing drifted past them, and they encountered a freezing blast that sliced into them. They heard weird howls of anguish and pain during the night but when the mist cleared there was nothing to see. One of the most terrifying scenarios they witnessed was that of a massive volcano that was situated in front of them. Hot ash rained down on them, but they escaped unscathed. They travelled onwards to the land of milk and honey and they finally reached their destination.

Garth mounted the staircase and then hurtled up the path and was gasping for breath when he reached the offices of Original Worlds. The tall figure of Daniel Chinn the CEO of Original Worlds rose to his feet as he entered his office.

"Greetings and well done. You will be a well-known megastar when the film comes out. Our new innovative slogan will be Original Worlds, a voyage into the unknown to amaze and terrify the traveller."

"Yeah, well those special effects were utterly amazing when that giant hand reached out and flipped the dragon. We were all spellbound. Then there were all these scary monsters such as the snort slicer and the worm crusher, no doubt inventions of your vivid imagination. By the way, the rest of the crew will be here shortly, they are trudging their weary way up the hill".

"OK, we have arranged lots of food and drink for them. It looks like we have a perfect wrap," said Chinn.

Ad Infinitum.

GOGO FISH

He was of rather large proportions, at least he thought that he was. However, unfortunately, he had nothing else to compare himself with. He had ascertained that he was definitely a male in his species. He had also discovered that he was a space traveller and had found himself embedded in a large rocky substance as he hurtled through space. His space vehicle was in fact an enormous meteorite that was heading for a distant galaxy. Yet somehow, he knew that he was part of a far larger picture in the distant future. Thousands of years before, the meteorite in which he was voyaging, was part of a vast meteorite that was split asunder. This was because it collided with another meteorite that was in orbit around a planet known as Earth. The collision hurled his meteorite far out into space where he continued his epic journey. He encountered several massive worlds. These planets had the effect of attracting his meteorite to them through their intense gravity and then hurling him far out into space caused by the planet's rotation. The whole process was repeated on numerous occasions. Although time had no meaning to him, as he meandered on through the galaxies, he did have occasional thoughts about the planet Earth and supposed that he was lucky to have survived.

He then decided that it was time to create an identity for himself. Many choices of a name came flooding into his head. After much deliberation, he decided to call himself Chip. He then found that by experimentation, it was possible to control the direction that the meteorite was heading. However, Chip found it almost impossible to control the frantic speed that they had attained. Millennium after millennium, he continued his journey and there was no respite. Chip was able to marvel at the incredible worlds that they passed. A couple of worlds had at least five moons, that circled trapped by their intense gravity. A cataclysmic explosion appeared in the night sky ahead of Chip, it was most probably an exploding gas giant. He foraged on through rainbow star systems that bathed his meteorite with hues of a multitude of colours. Then for no apparent reason, his craft slowed down dramatically. Then it came to a grinding halt as they plunged into the water. Obviously, they had landed in some kind of water world.

Chip felt no kind of apprehension as he discovered that he was able to breathe quite normally as he exited from his rocky domain. As he peered through the water that had engulfed him on all sides, he was amazed at the clarity of it. Chip then broke the surface and emerged in an ocean of tranquillity. In his subconscious, he registered the colour as emerald-green. He had also discovered that with one flick of his tail he was able to propel himself forward at a fantastic speed. In the waters around him there appeared to be little life. It was then that Chip decided to investigate the planet even further. With a flick of his tail, he pierced the water and for a brief instant hung in the air. The emerald-green waters stretched on all sides of him and disappeared into the far horizon. However, as he projected his vision still further a speck of something minute appeared. Chip then continued with his experimentation and realised that he was able to project his vision even further. Then this vast structure loomed out of the waters in front of him. Although he was not conversant with the word mountain, that was what it was. There was also something strange about the mountain, it seemed to be spewing forth some dark smoky material. Then Chip projected his vision even further and it materialised into high definition. Fiery projectiles were launched towards him forcing him to duck. The volcano then exploded into dramatic action, causing tremors to race across the previously tranquil waters. Chip's world had developed into a world of danger and menace. Some hidden instinct led him in the direction of the angry volcano and the seething waters that surrounded it.

"Hello and without being too personal what kind of creature are you? We don't appear to be of the same species" queried a voice.

As the voice had entered his head without invitation Chip was uncertain of where it had arrived from.

"Where exactly are you positioned? I have no idea where you are located" demanded Chip.

"Well, as you seem to be a good-natured creature I will show you," said the voice.

Then materialising in Chip's vision was the most perfect creature that he could ever imagine. She was a starburst of amazing colours with a delicate beak and feathers that twinkled with a myriad of colours.

"Thank you for your compliments, I love your thought that I am the most perfect creature that you could ever imagine," said the voice.

"So not only can you project your thoughts you can read mine as well. You really are a superior type of being. What species do you derive from and what is your name?" inquired Chip.

"My species is known as avian and unfortunately I don't believe that I have a name" replied the voice.

"Well, that is no problem at all. I shall create a name for you. I shall call you Twinkle" stated Chip.

"Yes, I like that name you may call me that," said Twinkle.

"However, as we are in the naming game, I shall respond by creating one for you "replied Twinkle.

"There is absolutely no need for that, I am called Chip" he replied.

"Ok you have a name then, what species do you derive from?" questioned Twinkle.

"Well, there again it's an incredibly long tale. I originally was part of a massive meteorite that collided with another meteorite that was in orbit around a planet that was called planet Earth. As a result of the collision half, the meteorite sheared off and plunged down onto planet Earth. Then I was subjected to an incredibly long never-ending journey that lasted for thousands of years. I often wondered what became of the other creature in the meteorite that plunged down to Earth, and did it survive. In reply to your question, what species am I, I'm a fish or to be more precise a Gogo fish" replied Chip.

"Then, will you be my companion, I have an instinct that we may need each other on the long journey ahead. That massive structure in the far distance is a volcano, so I have just been informed. It seems to be rather active and dangerous. Shall we head towards it?" questioned Twinkle.

"Yes, as they say, nothing ventured nothing gained. How do you intend to travel there? Being a rather inept fish, my only way of travel is by swimming. You, on the other hand, being an avian have presumably the power of flight," said Chip.

"Well, I suppose that there is a first time for everything and to be honest I have never tried to fly before," said Twinkle.

Then she immediately flapped her powerful wings and soared up into the blazing sky toward the distant volcano. Twinkle was a joy to behold as she gained momentum in her flying abilities. She plunged down on Chip forcing him to dive beneath the waters. Twinkle was giggling inanely as she completed the manoeuvre.

"That wasn't very funny. You could have severely maimed yourself by playing the idiot" Chip projected his thought.

"That is precisely why I am infatuated with you. You always play the supreme gallant, protecting his lady love "replied Twinkle.

"Yes, you are correct in your assumption. I wouldn't want anything to damage your perfect beauty" Chip retorted.

As they progressed, toward the volcano Twinkle was aloft and acting as the spy in the sky. She reported that there were some strange ungainly creatures that were flying in her direction. She then went on to report that the creatures whatever they were, had started to explode in front of her.

"Well, that is totally weird, it may have been something that disagreed with their digestion that they had consumed over lunch," said Chip.

As they continued with their journey in the direction of the volcano, they encountered even more anomalies. As Chip was swimming at a prodigious speed he was forced to come to a sudden stop. The reason for his abrupt halt was that he had encountered a mountainous wall of jelly that barred him from progressing any further. He endeavoured to communicate with it but received no response. Then he decided that the jelly mountain must be an inanimate object. Twinkle's response was most unexpected.

"Have you tried to eat it? Jelly is meant to be delicious," said Twinkle.

"I have no desire to sample something that will taste disgusting, besides which it may suddenly come to life and bite me" was Chip's instant response.

Then in both their shared interests of exploration and adventure, they agreed to differ. Then in the sky in front of her appeared numerous objects that were approaching at a significant speed. Twinkle reported this event to Chip who was situated in the waters below.

"My suggestion would be to carry on in the same direction until you are able to analyse if these creatures present a threat. It may be that these avians are perfectly amicable and have no hostile intentions whatsoever," said Chip.

They proceeded onwards in their search for fame and glory. Apparently, the avians had dramatically slowed down their speed, which Twinkle reported to Chip.

"As you are a solitary avian they are probably assessing if you present any danger to them. Are you able to estimate yet how many are there and their approximate size relative to yours?" Queried Chip.

"Well, in answer to your first question there must be at least a couple of hundred of them. However, regarding size and stature, I am fifty times larger than they are" replied Twinkle.

"Then it's no wonder that they paused. You probably cut a terrifying figure in their eyes" said Chip.

Then Twinkle invaded his mind with an alarming message. "These avians are now moving towards me at a very fast rate."

Some five hundred metres below her Chip panicked as there was nothing he could do to protect her from the multitude of avians whose sole intention must be to kill her. Then an extraordinary thing started happening to him. Although he was still underwater, his body started stretching. Everything inside him was changing and was absolute agony. On both sides of him, what had been his pectoral fins were now altering into wing-like protuberances. Still, the transfiguration continued, his body lengthened and lightened. He flapped the mighty wings that he had been endowed with and rose rapidly to the surface. He exploded from the water world's grasp and soared up into the air and into the midst of an aerial battle. However, the creatures that he emerged to do battle with were more like repulsive insects that had long stings thrust out in front of them.

Twinkle was just about holding her own against the frenzied attack of her enemies when Chip arrived during the mayhem, he attacked with such savagery that he blew them apart. The attackers desperately tried to regroup but by then it was far too late. They fled in all directions defeated and crushed with their stings between their legs.

Twinkle had been so busy coping with her own survival that she was unaware of Chip's intervention. When at last she glanced at him, she didn't recognize him and demanded to know who he was.

"So, you really don't recognise me, even after all that we have endured together. I am Chip, purportedly the love of your life" he told her.

Then if a stunning avian had the power to blush she would have surely done so.

"Your Chip," she said in an endearing manner.

"I know I am" was his instant response.

It was then that Twinkle informed Chip about the horrors that she had been forced to endure whilst being attacked by the malevolent insects. Apparently, they taunted her with the fact that their stings were coated with a deadly poison and once stung she would suffer an extremely painful death.

"Then, miraculously you appeared in your new guise as my saviour. When I state that you have changed dramatically that would be an understatement. You are now twice my size adorned with a magnificent pair of wings. You were once a fish but now somehow you can fly as well. What happened to you?" said Twinkle.

"Well, it is incredibly difficult to explain what exactly happened to me, but I must have had an Epiphany. I was underwater feeling totally helpless and realised with all my inner being, that I must save you from any harm, no matter the consequences. Almost immediately a transformation took place and eventually I became the creature that you see before you," said Chip.

"Yeah, and what a force of nature you have turned out to be. Believe it or not, I much prefer you in your current state as a winged champion to defend my honour" replied Twinkle.

"Then, our unbreakable relationship must continue. Those monstrous insects seemed to have dispersed in all directions. Somehow, I have this instinct that we should still head in the direction of the volcano," said Chip.

"Yes, that makes sense, and it is still a huge distance away. Which mode of transport do you intend to travel by? I thoroughly recommend the aerial route. It's far more scenic and we can indulge in polite conversation" replied Twinkle.

"Yes, my watery mode of transport would be a tad boring and lacking in stimulation. I shall therefore accept your kind offer and travel by the scenic route. This also has the added advantage of indulging in polite conversation. Or perhaps you want to keep an eye on me, to make sure that I don't stray off the beaten path," said Chip.

"Well, we can carry on conversing to while away the time or set off towards the volcano with a direct purpose in mind. The choice is entirely yours," said Twinkle.

Both carried on in the direction of the volcano. Although through the refraction of the light, they seemed to be not getting any nearer. The views that they encountered from their lofty position were eye-catching. On several occasions, they flew over strange and fearsome-looking creatures and Chip admitted that he was glad that he had taken the scenic route. At last, the volcano seemed to be getting nearer and they began to feel its effects on the waters that surrounded it. There were increasing tremors, that caused mountainous waves to crash into each other. This volcano was an amazing source of energy, and both began to feel the heat from its fiery crater. Eventually, as the heat became even more intense, they both decided to veer away from the volcano and continue in another direction. They had been flying for a couple of hours and began to feel quite jaded. They spotted a small island and descended onto it. The island appeared to be deserted and would be a good staging post for the next part of their journey.

"That's a most peculiar sensation I am sure the island moved" Twinkle exclaimed.

"Don't worry I just felt it as well "replied Chip.

Then both took off and hovered above the island. Then they watched in amazement as the island reared up upon four massive legs and trundled forward.

"I have just received a message in my mind informing me that the creature is a turtle Gargantua, and it is quite harmless," said Twinkle.

"Yeah, well lots of the information we receive is totally misleading. It's gigantic and I certainly wouldn't want it to sit on me. We seem to have extracted ourselves at precisely the correct time as it appears to be submerging under the waves" replied Chip.

"Well, I suppose that we should continue our journey and avoid alighting on suspicious objects that have a tendency to move" postulated Twinkle.

Heading away from the volcano there was an incredible drop in temperature, although it was still quite mild. Then as the temperature became balmy, they spotted another island. This was a far larger island than their previous encounter with the giant turtle, nevertheless, they circled it apprehensively before landing. They were astounded at the beauty of the multi-hued flowers that covered most of the island. The perfume of the flowers was so intense that they became soporific. For the first time, they realised that the island was populated by thousands of animals. The problem was that they were for the most part rotting corpses and cadavers. Chip quickly grabbed Twinkle and rose above the island.

"In my distant psyche, I know about these islands. They lure you into their embrace and you fall into a deep slumber never to wake up. They are affectionately known as dream islands. However, a more appropriate name would be death Island" informed Chip.

"Well, you have rescued me yet again from death by drug-induced slumber. To be honest I felt so relaxed and at peace with myself that I could have slept for a thousand years" replied Twinkle.

"Yeah, now let's travel onwards and see what further scrapes we get involved in," said Chip.

Large and forbidding cliffs started to form alongside them. The edge of the cliff was perpendicular and knife sharp. Then the blizzard struck, and they were hurtled over the cliffs into a meadow of grassland, which allowed them to make a soft landing.

"Well, that was exciting, and we could have ended up being splattered into those daunting cliffs, but at least we are fairly well sheltered here and safe for the time being," said chip.

A voice intruded into their thoughts.

"Don't be alarmed I am a pacifist and have not a voracious nature".

Where they had been sheltering it had been very misty, Now, as the mist cleared, they could identify an enormous creature with row after row of gleaming white teeth.

"You don't have the appearance of a pacifist unless those teeth are dentures. What kind of creature are you? You look like a cross between a dragon and a crocodile," said Twinkle.

"Both of you must realise that the island that you have just visited was filled with hallucinogenic properties. Therefore, you visualise me with fear and trepidation. Because of your visit to the island of dreams, your image of me has been thoroughly misplaced. Concentrate and I will no more be a figment of your imagination but a true reflection of myself" said the dragon figure.

Then, in front of both travellers, the transfiguration took place. The huge dragon-like figure shrank to minute proportions, the only thing about him that hadn't changed was the gleaming white teeth.

"Well, you really are a complete surprise. From a fearsome dragon-like creature, you have transformed into a minute harmless little person," said Twinkle.

"Yeah, this only goes to show that a drug-fuelled existence certainly impairs the mind. However, you are a decidedly friendlier person than your previous image. My next question must be, where are we and where do we go from here?" questioned Chip.

"Well, I can honestly say that your future is entirely up to you. However, your first question 'where are we?', has far more relevance. You are standing on the threshold of the creation star. This enables your imagination to reign supreme. If you require wealth and perhaps a royal crown, your wish will be granted. You seem like a happy couple, why don't you take a marital pledge and become King and Queen?" said the dragon figure.

It is rumoured, that in a star system a trillion lightyears from Earth, there once lived a King and Queen called Chip and Twinkle who went on to establish a mighty dynasty. They begat many offspring to carry on with the good works that had been instilled in them by their distant ancestors. There is absolutely no reason to think that the good works of this dynasty are not being carried on in perpetuity.

Ad Infinitum.

Authors note:
The go-go fish exists and is closely related to a catfish. A 380-million-year-old fish fossil was recently found in Kimberley in Western Australia. This fish contained many organs to be found in the human body. The 380 million years old heart is a prime example of this extraordinary coincidence.

PEST

Can you hear that mosquito when you are lying in bed?
Launching an attack on your arm leg or head.
That high-pitched wine with its jet-powered dive.
Flinching with fear when will it arrive?
I'm boiling and sweating, so I throw the sheets in the air.
its stung me ten times it's simply not fair!

ODE TO ALFIE

If you look Alfie up on a browser, it informs you that Alfie's a schnauzer.
Yes, he is whiskered with beard and likes to be feared but we know he's a terrible mouser.
Alfie likes to be petted and hates to be vetted and loves all his doggy friends.
They all race through the fields, as though they are on wheels and Alfie's

superb on the bends.

He is loyal but possessive and seldom aggressive and loves his little friend Albie as well.

But with his sensitive nose, we think and suppose that Alfie may think Albie's a rose.

Alfie is alpha that rhymes with alfalfa and plenty to do with our plot.

He is looking for treats, doggy type sweets, so off on his search he will trot.

He is the boss you will see, as he carries on his exciting quest for Holly and V.

He will point with his paw which is hard to ignore and then will piss on a tree.

He is cuddly and funny and will expose all his tummy, to be tickled again and again.

If it is cloudy and wet and he shows no regret, to hide under your car from the rain.

Alfie is great and he is our best mate he is as happy as happy as can be.

So well done you girls, happiness is worth more than gold, or all the pearls in the sea.

THE WEATHER

You never know what the weather brings a sunny day when nature sings.
Or torrential rains with floods that block the drains, delaying both the cars and trains.
The sun blazes down across the sand while children frolic across the strand.
Then a gale blows up from who knows where? the winds are vast it is just not fair.
We travel by boat far out to sea sixty-foot waves are not for me.
The seasons change we do not know why? sometimes it is wet sometimes it's dry.
Our travel plans are made to go, but we cannot get out because of snow.
To make it worse I just fell down an icy patch across the ground.
If you have a depression in the weather system, it sounds bad and makes you sad.
Yet if you have a high in the weather system it sounds spry and makes you fly.
Climate change is our demise which increases thoughts to our unease.
What causes climate change I hear you ask? we should curtail it now must be our task.
Across our planet it has warmed by one degree or more, the exact figure I am not sure.
The oceans are mounting to swamp the land, to drown in shit is, not so grand.
It's humanity's lifestyle you must blame, in oil and gas there lies the shame.
While ice sheets melt and the planet heats, we still indulge in lifestyle treats.
In the mighty oceans that surround our earth, another danger has given birth.
Plastic a product derived from stinking oil poisons the oceans there is no recoil.

Fish expire from a diet of plastic, having entered the food chain it can be quite drastic.
then where do we go have you got a solution? yes, I have, back in time to the industrial revolution.
we will travel back in our time machine and expunge all industry that is our dream.
what about progress and invention? That just will not happen is my intention.

A LEAFS LIFE

I tremble and curl where once I was once different.
My memories are sap-filled lithe and dart-like.
Light as air and above the seas of windblown clouds.
Twisted and turned me to their indomitable will.
Before that, I remember little.
Perhaps I was formed as a microcosm of a mighty titan.
That bore a thousand such as me.
But now as the seasons change.
Colours turn to browns and reds.
I tumble and fall to be trampled underfoot.
I cease to exist, but I am still aware.

THE SOLITARY FLY

I am a fly. You may see me fly by, people tend to shun me, and I don't know why.
I have many brothers and sisters that hang around in crowds, but I prefer freedom which is up there in the clouds.
My relations that stretch across many nations are fascinated by smells, I am enamoured with the country as I drift across the fells.
I hate the stench of dying things that linger in the air, the graveyard odours are not for me, and warn me to beware.
A monstrous bluebottle has just flown past, got crushed by a lorry he was going too fast.
There are other insects not like me, wasps with stings and the honeybee.
Beautiful insects are there too, dragonflies and the alpine blue.
Sometimes I do feel lonely as I do not have a friend it's a lonely road, I wander up will it never end?.
Tedium is not a medium that I embrace, to enjoy the company of a lady fly is not a disgrace.
Where would I find this insect of my dreams, perhaps she is hiding in the sky behind a cluster of moonbeams.
Then out of the corner of my multifaceted eye, I sense the image of an attractive lady fly.
She floats towards me on her elegant gossamer wings, her perfume is intense and all the world sings.
Will she like me? I don't know, I am quite small, but I will grow.
She is dainty, I can see, I can see that she is the lady fly for me.
My quest has ended I have found my love, she just descended from the sky above.

THE SOLITARY FLY

Then disaster strikes as it is often said, she had alighted on a path where humans tread.
These humans' feet have enormous spread, one landed on my lady love and she became dead.
I know that I may search for a thousand years, but I will never find another like her, they are my fears.
A solitary fly I may be, when you are alone just think of me!

HIS RAGE

It bubbled up inside him an intense uncontrollable rage.
He was seething with anger and trapped in a cage.
He paced up and down and exploded with fury.
His desire was intense for fame and international glory.
He simmered with anger and his features became red.
He shouted and screamed I wish I was dead.
What have I achieved in my long wasteful life??
The wars continue around me and trouble and strife.
I search for redemption the ultimate prize.
Which is only obtained by the good and wise..

LOCKDOWN

WHO ARE THESE PEOPLE WHO CREATE THE LAW? THEIR DRACONIAN MEASURES ARE HARD TO IGNORE.
THEY HAVE LOCKED DOWN OUR COUNTRY WITH INDISCRIMINATE HASTE, BIG BROTHER IS HERE WE WILL GIVE YOU A TASTE.
IS IT LOCKDOWN OR KNOCKDOWN? IT JUST FEELS THE SAME, WE ARE PROTECTING YOU ALL IT'S NOT US YOU BLAME.
WE ARE THE GOVERNMENT YOU SEE AND WE THRIVE ON SUCCESS THROUGH THE WONDERFUL ENDEAVOURS WE SEEK TO IMPRESS.
OUR MEDICAL KNOWLEDGE IS FORTHRIGHT AND CLEAR, WE BASE IT ON STATS THERE IS NO NEED TO FEAR.
OUR INTENTION IS PREVENTION OF THIS PESTILENT SCOURGE, WE ARE LOCKING YOU DOWN PAY ATTENTION WE URGE.
WE ARE THE LORDS OF HAVOC AND DOOM, WE DISCOURAGE ANY LAUGHTER WE PROMOTE ONLY GLOOM.
WE ARE SHUTTING ALL RESTAURANTS, THUS BANNING ALL FOOD, FUN TAKES THE BACK SEAT AND WE THINK THIS IS GOOD.
WE ARE DOLING OUT MONEY TO KEEP FIRMS AFLOAT IF YOU FEEL YOU ARE SINKING JUMP OUT OF THE BOAT.
MY REPLY IS, THE GOVERNMENT THINKS WE ARE STUPID AND LAX, THE MONEY IS OURS FROM PAST PAID INCOME TAX.
THEY STOP US FROM TRAVELLING AND GOING AFAR, THIS ISN'T A PLANE IT'S ONLY A CAR.
HOW IONG WILL IT LAST I HEAR YOU ALL SAY? THEY REPLY WE DON'T REALLY KNOW NOT FOREVER WE PRAY.
WHERE CAN WE ESCAPE TO AVOID ALL THIS MESS, THERE'S NOWHERE ON EARTH I HEARD YOU JUST STRESS.

CAN IT GET ANY WORSE? I THOUGHT I WOULD DECRY LIKE CHRISTMAS IS CANCELLED HEARD FROM A SPY.
THEN WHO IS THE PERPETRATOR IN THIS GHASTLY GAME? ITY'S SILLY LITTLE BORIS THEY ALL EXCLAIM.
AD INFINITUM.

Made in United States
North Haven, CT
07 March 2023